QUEENS

OF

FENNBIRN

Also by Kendare Blake

Novels
Three Dark Crowns
One Dark Throne
Anna Dressed in Blood
Girl of Nightmares
Antigoddess
Mortal Gods
Ungodly

Digital Novellas
The Young Queens
The Oracle Queen

Novella Collection
Queens of Fennbirn

QUEENS

OF

FENNBIRN

KENDARE BLAKE

HARPER TEEN

An Imprint of HarperCollinsPublishers

HarperTeen is an imprint of HarperCollins Publishers.

Queens of Fennbirn
Copyright © 2018 by Kendare Blake
All rights reserved. Printed in the United States of America.
No part of this book may be used or reproduced in any manner whatsoever
without written permission except in the case of brief quotations embodied
in critical articles and reviews. For information address HarperCollins
Children's Books, a division of HarperCollins Publishers, 195 Broadway,
New York, NY 10007.
www.epicreads.com

ISBN 978-0-06-274828-7

Typography by Aurora Parlagreco
18 19 20 21 22   PC/LSCH   10 9 8 7 6 5 4 3 2 1
❖
First Edition

CONTENTS

————— ✤ ◊ ⚜ —————

THE

YOUNG

QUEENS

PROLOGUE:
THE BLACK COTTAGE

⚜

*T*he day of the birth of the queens who would come to be known as Mirabella, Arsinoe, and Katharine was still, unremarkable, and without omens. There was no great wind to howl the arrival of an elemental queen. No bloody fish kill against the rocks to signal the coming of the war gift. All across Fennbirn—from the capital of Indrid Down to the smallest villages—elders and the dwindling number of seers cast divinations and downed trance potions, only to pass out drunk and see the oracle bones lie on the ground in nonsense patterns. The triplets were born, in silence and in private, with only the queen, the king-consort, and the Midwife to bear witness.

Three black witches, the mainland would say. Born to a descending queen. One would rise to become queen in her place. Perhaps the strongest of the three. Perhaps the cleverest. Or perhaps it would be the girl born under the best shield of luck.

"It was an easy labor," said the Midwife. "You were lucky, Queen Camille."

"Easy," Camille said, and scoffed, "Easy for you to say, Willa." But even though she hurt, and ached, and could barely keep her eyes open, she knew it could have gone worse. From the moment her pregnancy was known, her foster sister Genevieve Arron had filled her head with tales of births gone wrong. On Camille's last day at the Volroy, just before she departed for the Black Cottage to give birth, Genevieve spoke of so much blood and screaming that Camille had nearly passed out. She had stopped short and stood frozen, as if standing still would somehow stop the triplets from coming. She did not move until her eldest foster sister, Natalia, had taken her by the arm and walked her to the coach.

"Do not let her frighten you, Camille," Natalia had said. "Queens have birthed the triplets for thousands of years."

"But not all have survived," Genevieve had continued to taunt. "I was only trying to prepare her, so that she might see the signs of it going wrong. So that she might fight for her life."

Genevieve. Younger than the queen and completely spoiled, and always as mean as the snakes they kept to adorn themselves with at parties.

Camille lay back in the birthing bed, remembering her last days at the Volroy, as Willa pressed a cool cloth to her forehead.

"Well," said Willa, and brushed the queen's black hair out of her eyes, "you are breathing, aren't you?"

Camille looked at the bassinets across the room, each with

a sleeping queen inside. The firstborn, Mirabella the elemental, had come in such a rush, with such electricity to her that Camille had shouted her gift before her name. Elemental Mirabella. Arsinoe the poisoner had arrived not long after; Willa had barely gotten Mirabella washed and settled into her blankets. But sweet little naturalist Katharine had given her a rest, taking so long that they feared her sisters would start to fuss.

"I did it," Camille said as her eyes began to close. "I survived. And now my reign is over."

When she woke, the three bassinets were gone, whisked away by Willa to the nursery down the hall. In their place was a chair, and slumped down on it, snoring softly, was her king-consort, Philippe.

Sweet Philippe. He had won her hand in the Hunt of the Stags, when she could not choose her favorite from the suitors that the Arrons approved of. Sometimes she thought it was the only bit of luck that the Goddess ever gave her. Though he had little power in the face of the Arrons, he had loved Camille well, and a life away from the island with him was all she had ever looked forward to. When her triplets came after only seven years of her rule, she was overjoyed.

They would leave now, and trade the island for the world. Out there, she would be just a woman, free to make her own path. All she had to give up was her crown, and that she had already torn off her head and thrown during the births.

Camille looked around the room. Willa had done a fine job

of cleaning while she slept. The bloody cloths and trays of sharp knives were gone, the cloths burned and the knives returned to storage in case the next queen's birth was not so lucky and the triplets needed to be cut out. Mellow incense smoke cleared the stench of sweat and labor, and she had set a warm, crackling fire in the fireplace.

Outside, the December night was dark—only the faintest hint of moonlight reflected across the snowdrifts. Camille gingerly swung her leg over the edge of the bed and winced. She took a moment to collect herself, held her sagging, empty belly with one arm and swung the other until she stood. Her vision wavered, and for a moment, she feared Philippe would wake to the sound of her collapsing on the floor. But the weakness passed. She slipped a blanket about her shoulders like a shawl, and walked out.

"Where are you going, my love?" Philippe, more awake than she had thought, grasped her wrist softly as she passed. "You should be resting. We have a long journey tomorrow." His eyes lingered on her pale face, and then on the floor, and on the small trail of dripped blood she left behind.

She patted him, and he let go. His heavily lidded eyes blinked shut. He was, even after years on the island, still a mainland man and trusted that she must know best about these women's mysteries.

"I am only going to look in on them."

"Shall I go with you?"

She shook her head. Philippe was a strong consort, but he

was too softhearted for this. If he saw the triplet queens, he might want to hold them. And if he held them, he might start to feel that they were his instead of Fennbirn's.

Queen Camille walked down the high-ceilinged hall of the Black Cottage, one hand out along the wall to steady her. The light from the lamps in the nursery cast warm yellow light, and inside, another bright fire crackled against the cold.

Much like Camille's king-consort, Willa slept upright in a chair. Though not, perhaps, as prettily. Willa's mouth hung open, and her head fell over to the side. Her snore sounded like a pig searching excitedly for mushrooms.

Camille crept past. The newborn queens in the bassinets were dressed in black and affixed with the colors of their gifts. Blue buttons for elemental Mirabella, and a purple patch for poisoner Arsinoe. Pretty green ribbons for tiny naturalist Katharine. Even the bassinets had been decorated with items associated with each gift: a cloud-shaped pillow, a mobile hung with snakes and spiders, and a quilt embroidered with flowers.

"Enjoy the colors, little queens," Camille whispered. "Soon enough it will all be black, black, black."

She looked down on their sleeping faces—red and wrinkled, and angry-looking, even at birth. She did not blame them. Their lives would not be easy. And then two lives would be over.

Camille was a poisoner, like Queen Nicola, and Queen Sylvia before her. Three generations of poisoner queens. Almost a dynasty. But instead of growing stronger, it seemed that the blood of the poisoner queens grew thinner. The Arrons flourished in their power, as well as other poisoner families in Prynn and the capital, but Sylvia was stronger than Nicola, and Camille was the weakest of all. Over hundreds of years, the other gifts of the island had lessened: elementals lost their mastery over one or more elements, and the war-gifted lost the ability to guide their weapons with their minds. The naturalists' familiars grew smaller and smaller. And the oracles . . . The true oracle gift was almost gone, thanks to generations of drowned oracle queens.

Something was changing on the island and within the line of queens. As a queen, Camille could feel that. Not that anyone would believe her. The Arrons never listened when she spoke of queenly instinct. They never listened to her about anything. They had been bullies her whole life, from the moment they claimed her from that very cottage. They shamed her when she failed. They did not let her rule. With each successive poisoner queen, the queen herself mattered less and less. The line of queens was not important, the Arrons said. It was the poisoners who the Goddess truly favored.

In their bassinets, the new triplets hummed with an aura of the gift each carried, that energy—like a scent or a heartbeat— that linked them to the Goddess and called to the queensblood in Camille. It was that which told her what she had given birth to, when she announced it to Willa, and named them, as though in a trance. It *was* like a trance. On Arsinoe and Katharine, the auras that lingered were weak. On Katharine it was barely a hint. But Mirabella still blazed with it.

"What are you doing here, Queen Camille?"

Camille flinched. Willa's voice from behind her had sounded like Mistress Arron.

"Nothing." She straightened her shoulders as Willa rose from her chair and came slowly to join her. "Only looking in on them. The messengers have been dispatched?" Messengers, summoned to the Black Cottage upon her labor, to ferry word to Rolanth, Indrid Down, and Wolf Spring. The elemental, poisoner, and naturalist cities, respectively.

"They have. They rode out at dusk."

Camille sucked in her cheeks. A messenger to Indrid Down was hardly necessary anymore. The poisoners were so assured of their destiny.

Camille nodded to the baby in the storm-blue blanket.

"Her, there. Mirabella. She will be the next queen."

Willa, still a servant of her temple teachings though no longer a priestess, made a pious gesture, touching first her eyes and then her heart.

"The Goddess decides," Willa said. "Only she decides who rules her island."

Camille took a deep breath. The walls of the cottage where the queens would spend their first six years, where she spent her own first six years, closed in, squeezing her out. Here they would play and have their hair braided. Here they would learn to walk and run, and if they were lucky, to not love one another too much.

"She decides," Camille said. "But the queen knows. And I was mistaken about those two." She pointed to poisoner Arsinoe and naturalist Katharine. "Arsinoe is a naturalist. Katharine . . . a poisoner." She almost said war-gifted, to deny the Arrons a queen at all. But they would never believe it. They would investigate and look too closely.

"Camille . . ." Willa turned to her, and shook her head.

Camille clenched her jaw. She was still bleeding, and exhausted. For all she knew, she was slowly dying. But she willed herself to look strong. To look like the queen she was, for once.

"Mirabella will be queen. I can see that. Feel that. And she will be a great one. These other two will not survive long. Katharine's gift is so weak, it will never fully quicken. And Arsinoe . . . Another poisoner queen will not sit the throne. But if the Arrons have a gifted poisoner, they will make her suffer. Training and belittling. Beating her when she gets it wrong. Like they did to me."

"And what would they do with Queen Katharine?" Willa asked.

"What could they do with a giftless girl but leave her alone?" Camille swallowed hard. That was a lie. The Arrons could do plenty to a giftless girl. Everything they ever did to Camille, and worse. But at least they would fail. At least they would have no winning queen.

She looked down at little Katharine. The child was doomed already. "Change the queens' gowns, Willa. So they are right."

Willa looked from Arsinoe to Katharine. "If Mirabella is the chosen queen, then it will not matter."

"It will not matter," Camille agreed. She had known Willa since she was a girl. Willa had been a young woman then, deep in her midwife training, when she presided over the births of Camille and her sisters, and she was the one who raised them. She showered them with sweets and games. And they were happy.

"You cared for me so well, Willa," said Camille. "You loved me."

"I loved you all."

"And you love me still." Camille pressed her lips together. Through the nightmares, and the screaming fits, and the black blanket of depression that coiled round and round a queen's neck as the birth neared. Through the days full of tremors, when Camille had tried to claw the babies out of her stomach. Willa was there. She brewed her teas to calm her. She told her it was normal. That the bearing of queens was always haunted by the fallen ones who came before, and the Black Cottage was full of ghosts. Even Camille's own poisoned sisters.

It was the first time Willa had spoken of Camille's sisters. After they were dead, fallen queens were never spoken of. They were forgotten, except by the families who had raised them, and the sister who survived. Camille had survived and become queen. Her sisters had not. The sisters of a true poisoner, they had died on the same day, in the same hour, writhing. Spitting blood.

"I love you still, and I will always, Camille," said Willa. "But I cannot do this."

"I am doing it." Camille lay her hand on her Midwife's shoulder. "I know that I took my crown off and threw it at you. But I am still the queen."

In the morning, Queen Camille and her king-consort readied themselves to leave the island. It was a strange thing, to pack her own trunks and to dress her own sore body. But she would get used to it.

"Are you sure you are well?" Philippe asked. He glanced at the spots of blood on the floor, the pool of blood in her bed that had soaked through her clothes and cloth padding. "Our ship home can wait, if you need to rest longer. They won't sail without us."

"We go today," Camille said. She felt weaker this morning than she had in the night, looking down on the new queens. But her time on the island was over. And she had done what she could to ease their paths.

It was not for them that you did it, her conscience amended. *It was for you and for revenge.*

"It was for the island," she muttered. And it was not a terribly fulfilling revenge, anyway, when she would not be there to see it.

"What did you say? Camille—"

"I am fine, I said. The bleeding is normal." She had begun to tremble slightly. The bleeding was a bit heavy, perhaps, but she was not sure. She had never birthed triplets before, after all.

Philippe watched her, then sighed and nodded. How relieved he would be to return to the world. His world, where men ruled. It gave her pause sometimes, wondering how he would change. He loved her on her island, but out there it might all be different. He might expect her to be something she had no idea how to be.

"I'll take these to the carriage," he said, and picked up the last of her cases. Camille followed, but she lingered in the hall near the open door of the nursery, where inside, Willa rocked and cooed to the new queens.

They said the old queen was glad to go. Glad to be done. That her queen-bearing, and her flight, was instinctual.

But when Camille looked at the babies, for just a moment she wished she had jaws like her beloved snakes, so she could unhinge them and swallow the girls back down under her heart forever.

"How can I go," she whispered.

"You'll forget," Willa said gently. "The moment your feet cross the threshold. With every step you take across the island. When you set foot into the boat. You'll forget."

"I . . . worry for them."

"Even though you know which one will be crowned?" Willa looked up; Camille looked away. Mirabella was the strongest child, true. And last night with the birthing blood rushing through her veins, she thought she had seen something in the little queen's future. Something chosen. But in the daylight she remembered that she was only a used-up vessel. She knew what the queens were, but their fates were their own. She was no oracle.

"Will you change them back, after I am gone?" Camille asked, and then a pain tore through her, and she cried out. Willa left the babies to their bassinets and came to hold her by the elbows.

"Your skin is cold," she said. She looked at Camille's face and embraced her suddenly, kissing her forehead. "I will do as my queen wishes."

THE DAY OF THE CLAIMING

———— ✿ ❦ ⚜ ————

Six Years Later

WOLF SPRING

❧

*J*uillenne Milone stares at the colors swirling through the pearl, plucked fresh from an unlucky oyster that morning. She holds it up to the sun to admire the greens and pinks and gentle golds. It is very beautiful, and truth be told, she would rather not give it up. But Aunt Caragh says an offering is no use if it is something you do not want anyway, so she purses her lips and chooses the spot, directly in the middle of her patch of yellow daffodils. She digs deep and buries the pearl, getting dirt on her cheeks and somehow managing to sprinkle some into her dark brown hair. She prays to bless the young queens she and her aunt Caragh depart from Wolf Spring to see today, because Aunt Caragh told her to.

For a moment, the soil under her palm pulses with heat, stronger than the sun shining down on her head, and she feels the Goddess of the island rush into her blood, making her one with everything the soil touches: the roots and the pearl and the

17

wind. And then the moment passes, and Jules gets to her feet.

Juillenne is six years old. Six and a half, really. She was born in December, like the queens themselves were, nine months after the Beltane fires. On the island, fall passes with heavy bellies painted for the reaping moon, in the hopes that babies conceived at Beltane will be nearly as strong as the queens. The Beltane Begots, those lucky children are called, and her grandpa Ellis says that bearing one was the only thing her mother, Madrigal, ever did by the island's rules. Even so, the magic did not take. Jules was born a pretty child, with one blue eye and one green, with tan skin and thick, dark curls. But she was also born small, and weak, and sick almost the second she breathed the air. A bad sign for a child born into the strongest family of naturalists on Fennbirn, who in three generations had had only half a dozen cases of illness to split among them.

Or so her grandparents say. Jules of course does not remember, any more than she remembers her mother, who left Jules and the island when Jules was three years old. Another unlucky sign.

Jules steps away from the daffodils and wipes the dirt from her hands onto her pants, on the sides and the back, so Aunt Caragh will not see. Behind her, the grass rustles, and her best friend, Joseph Sandrin, shoves her and says, "Boo!"

"I heard you coming," she says.

"Did not." He bends to inspect the spot where she buried the pearl, and Jules waits with held breath for his nod of approval. Even at six years old, she knows that something about Joseph is special. Something that is not like other boys, and her stomach clenches around the feeling—it is exciting and scary. Then he squints up at her, and whatever it was disappears, and he is just Joseph again.

"It was the one I said, wasn't it," he says.

"Maybe."

"It was. It was the oyster I chose. The one I brought you."

The oyster he brought her was delicious and salty, but it held no pearl. Though he was born to a mostly giftless family (his oldest brother Matthew is able to charm fish), Joseph thinks he has a touch of the sight gift, and no one on the island can convince him any different.

They stand together in her aunt Caragh's garden of radishes, green tomatoes, daffodils, and sunflowers. Two children with dirty trouser legs and matching blue shirts. Joseph and Jules, inseparable since birth.

"When do you have to go?" he asks.

"I don't know. Pretty soon." Jules looks back at the house. The season has started off hot, and Aunt Caragh's familiar, a lean brown hound named Juniper, lies in a patch of dirt to stay cool. It is only the four of them in the house now, only Jules and Aunt Caragh, Grandma Cait and Grandpa Ellis. Great-Grandma Sasha died in her sleep and was burned before the first snow. Her ashes feed the daffodils on which Jules and Joseph now stand. Jules reaches out and strokes a yellow, velvet petal. Birth and death and rebirth. These are words she knows, and she thinks with sudden panic that they are words she should understand. That somehow they are tied to this day and these queens in a way that is important.

"I don't know why you have to be the ones to take her," says Joseph. He has never much cared for change and has spent most of the last few weeks trying to figure a way out of Jules taking in another girl.

"Because she's a naturalist," says Jules. "And because we're the guardians."

"My ma and pa say that it doesn't look like she's anything."

"Well, Aunt Caragh says that's what being a naturalist looks like," she says, and shoves him.

Joseph scowls. "She won't be with us all the time," he says, half a question, half a demand, and looks at Jules with stormy blue eyes.

"Hardly at all. She's a queen. But we have to be kind to her."

"Because she's a queen."

Three dark queens are born in a glen. But only one will rule. Jules knows the rhyme by heart. But in her young mind it is only a rhyme. She has not thought about the other queens and who they are. Where they must go.

Aunt Caragh calls for Juillenne through an open window.

"Guess you have to go put on a dress," says Joseph. "Glad I don't have to."

"Me too," says Jules, and they laugh.

"Want to take the boat out and swim when you get back? Or we can just swim off the dock."

"I don't know. Aunt Caragh says the journey will take a long time. And when we get back, *she'll* be here."

Joseph frowns. "Well . . . you'll have to bring her along, then, I guess. She can't be that bad." He walks through the yard and waves when he gets to the edge of it, and Jules waves back. She can't be that bad, he says, but what does he know? The girl is a queen. Even though they say she is a naturalist, she could still be terrible.

Jules stretches her hand out toward the patch of blue oat grass that grows beside the daffodils, in the shade of the trees. For a moment, gentle energy moves from the center of her out to her fingertips, and she breathes in, unafraid, mostly impatient that she cannot ripen the fields yet like her grandparents or bloom a rose in her palm like Caragh.

The oat grass turns to her like she is the sun, but it grows no taller. Not yet. When she comes into the fullness of her gift, she will be able to grow a garden as lush as this one, with nothing more than wishes and coaxing. Grandpa Ellis says that the naturalist queen Bernadine, whose familiar the city of Wolf Spring was named for, could bring a field to harvest with a thought. But that was a long time ago, and besides, Jules is no queen.

"Juillenne!" Caragh shouts. "Stop dallying in the garden!"

Jules runs to the house and scoops up her grandpa Ellis's familiar-dog, Jake, to use as a furry white shield against Caragh's impatience.

THE BLACK COTTAGE

❧

Willa watches the young queens as they ready themselves in eldest triplet Mirabella's bedroom. Though the bedroom belongs to all of them, really. Neither Arsinoe nor Katharine has spent a full night in her own room since . . . well, since they traded their cradles for beds.

"No," says Arsinoe, and throws her formal black dress on the floor. "It does not fit right."

"It does so fit," says Mirabella. She takes it from little Katharine, who has retrieved it from the rug. "It fits how it is supposed to."

"You would know that if you ever wore one," Katharine adds, and sticks out her tongue.

The girls are being difficult. Katharine likes her dress but does not want to have her hair braided. Mirabella's hair is done, but she is unsatisfied with her sash. And Arsinoe . . . Arsinoe refuses everything.

That, Willa supposes, is her fault. She has raised them according to their designated gifts and let Arsinoe run wild in the woods. Let her tromp through the streambeds and dive after crayfish. Sweet Katharine has been primped and spoiled, and they have all looked upon her as their own special treasure. As for Mirabella, Willa remembers well the words of the queen. Mirabella is chosen. Strong. Born to rule. It shows in the way that she is with her sisters, always in charge of them and always the mediator. Or perhaps that, too, is due to how she was raised. Camille's prediction was impossible to forget. So even though she was not supposed to, Willa has groomed Mirabella over her sisters for the crown. As soon as the girl could read, Willa spent hours in the cottage library with her, poring over the history of the island.

But today is the day. Their claiming day, when the elemental, poisoner, and naturalist families will come to take their queens away. She has known forever that it was coming. But six years is a long time, full of long days of growth and laughter, and Willa has come to look at the queens as hers. Her queens. Her girls. More so even than she had with Queen Camille, perhaps because she is older now, and this generation will be her last.

"Queen Arsinoe, come to me."

Arsinoe does as she is told, trudging across the room to stand before Willa with her head hanging. Willa reaches out and wipes a streak of dirt from the little girl's cheek. Before the day is done Arsinoe will find a way to become filthy. She has such a knack for it that Willa half believes that Camille really did mistake her gift, and she truly is a naturalist made for digging in the soil.

"Raise your arms," Willa says. "Out of that shirt."

"May I wear trousers under the dress, at least?"

"No. Not today. But you are going home with the naturalists. Good working people, by the sea. You will like it there. And I doubt that they will make you dress too formally, except for on festival days."

Arsinoe sighs and lets Willa get her out of her clothes and into the dress with minimal tugging. When she is finished, the queen goes dutifully to her sister to have the tangles brushed out of her hair.

Perhaps due to the strain of the day, Katharine begins to cry, and it is hard for Willa not to comfort her. Mirabella and Arsinoe stop, as if they should turn and wrap her in their arms. But they do not. It is time for Katharine to learn to stand on her own, and after a moment, she quits crying and wipes her cheeks.

The Arrons will not be pleased with her. When the poisoner gift does not come, they may treat her even worse than they treated Queen Camille. Once, Willa feared what would happen as the queens grew and their families began to suspect they had been switched. But they will never come to suspect. Weak-gifted or giftless queens are no longer uncommon, where it is unheard of for a queen to be designated wrong at birth. And Willa should know. She has searched through the histories.

"Mirabella is chosen," Willa whispers, and makes a pious gesture, left over from her days as a young priestess, before she felt the Goddess pulling her into service at the Black Cottage. "And if she is chosen, the other gifts will not matter."

They may never even be an issue. Neither Arsinoe nor Katharine has shown the slightest hint of a gift, not their true ones or any other, whereas Mirabella's elements showed when she was four years old. Perhaps sooner than that, but that was when Willa first saw her playing with the candle flames: putting them out and lighting them again with her tiny, pointed finger. Other elements followed after: a tremor in the ground when she was frightened, or overcast skies when she is nervous like today.

So it seems that Queen Camille was right.

Katharine, eyes dry, steps up to the mirror beside her sisters and quickly organizes the brushes and combs and bits of ribbon on the dresser. She is such a pretty, delicate queen. And somehow sweet despite being spoiled.

"You look odd with your hair like that," she says to Arsinoe.

"You look odd *all the time*," Arsinoe says back, and Mirabella tugs on her braid.

"No fighting." Mirabella reaches for a length of black ribbon. "This is our last day together."

"But we will see each other sometimes. At festivals," says Arsinoe.

"We will see one another when we are all grown up," Mirabella corrects her. "That is what Willa said. When we are tall."

"Then we will never see Kat again. She will never be tall."

"And you will never be smart!" Katharine hisses, and Mirabella laughs. They are so different, in character and in feature. Arsinoe's scowl was apparent from the age of two. When Mirabella lost her baby cheeks, her fine bones and slender neck made her look every bit the oldest. And Katharine's large, heavily lashed eyes were impossible to miss. Willa has not needed to use colored cords or buttons to tell them apart since they could crawl.

"What if we do not like them?" Katharine asks. "The people who come to take us?"

"You will," Mirabella says. "You are going to Indrid Down. The capital city! Someday we will visit you there, and you must show us all around it."

Willa turns to leave them alone. The families will arrive soon, and she must still get ready herself. The young queens' laughter rings out and follows her down the hall.

"Have this, your last day as sweet girls," she whispers. "For when you next meet, you will remember none of it."

THE CLAIMING

———————— ❧ ————————

*J*ules follows Aunt Caragh down the seldom-used path through the Greenwood that leads to the Black Cottage, where the queens are born. The path is not well-groomed, and brambles and prickers catch on the hem of her black skirt, and scratch against the leather of her boots. When they get back to the carriage, she will have to pick bits of plant from Juniper's floppy ears and the pads of her paws.

"Keep up, Jules," says Aunt Caragh, and Juniper turns and woofs. Jules does her best, a small girl on small legs—nothing like her aunt or even like the photos she has seen of her mother, Madrigal. Everyone in Wolf Spring talks about those Milone girls, with their shining light brown hair and swaying limbs like a willow's branches. It makes Jules wonder who her short, dark father was and resent him a little.

In the carriage, Caragh had changed into her best black dress, the modest one with the high collar and shining buttons.

She anointed her wrists and forehead with oil and swept her hair high off her neck, and though the rest of the family says that Madrigal is far prettier, to Juillenne, Caragh is very beautiful. Jules tried to do her hair like her aunt's, but it was too wild and wavy. It fell out of its pins, and Jules feels ugly, and tied tight by the fastenings of her dress.

"Why didn't we take the carriage to the Black Cottage?" she asks.

"Because the claiming is held in the high meadow," Caragh replies. "And because this is queen business and all ritual. We must come from different directions and take them away in different directions."

"That's stupid."

"Aye, and you're not the only one who thinks so." Caragh turns and smiles out of the side of her mouth. "But hold your tongue when we get there. They'll be angry enough as it is that it's you and I who have come, instead of your grandma Cait."

Jules nods. She tries not to think ahead to the Black Cottage and what they will find there, instead daydreaming about returning to Wolf Spring, getting out of the hot, scratchy dress and into the cold, fresh water of Sealhead Cove, near Joseph's house. On bright days she can see clear to the rocky bottom.

"Caragh!"

They turn to see a tall boy following them down the path, shaking leaves out of his hair and brushing dust off his vest and slacks. It is Matthew, Joseph's brother, older than him by a full eleven years. Jules shouts his name and runs up the path to jump into his arms, and he tickles her belly until she is breathless.

"Matthew!" Caragh exclaims. "What are you doing here?"

"I missed you. So I waited a day and followed on horseback."

"But you aren't supposed to be here. And put my niece down. She's had too much Sandrin influence already, cavorting with Joseph." Despite her tone, Caragh goes and kisses Matthew's cheek.

"She's not the only Milone with a weakness for Sandrin boys," he says.

"What's 'cavorting'?" asks Jules.

"Nothing," both adults answer together.

"What are you doing here, Matthew?" Caragh asks. "I mean really."

"I really did miss you," he says. "And I couldn't let you show up alone. Not with the grand crowds and caravans the Arrons and the Westwoods will be towing."

"So Jules and I together is a shame, but you and I and Jules is not?"

"One Sandrin makes all the difference."

"You know, there's always the chance we could miss them. I didn't push the horses to hurry through the mountains."

Matthew shakes his head. "The sisters leave at the same time." He bends down to Jules and makes a face. "Pulled apart screaming, like they're pulling clots from wet wounds."

"Matthew, that's only a story," scolds Caragh as Jules giggles. "And a terrible one."

"Jules can handle it. She has picked her share of scabs. And if you wanted to shield her, you shouldn't have brought her."

The wind picks up and rushes through the trees, cold from coming down the face of Mount Horn and through the glen. It rattles branches and sends leaves flying past Jules's cheeks.

"Seems like the Westwoods are just arriving."

Maybe it is the elemental gift, or maybe it is only a spring breeze, but it makes Jules feel very insignificant suddenly, and she tugs on Caragh's long, flowing skirt.

"Don't be afraid, Squirt," says Matthew. "That and one lonely rain cloud probably exhausted half the Westwood clan." But as he finishes speaking, a great bolt of lightning cracks through the sky and touches the rocky summit of the mountain.

Caragh scoops Jules up and plants her on her hip. They walk fast toward the Black Cottage and the high meadow without another word. Jules cannot help but cry, though she does so as softly as she can.

They reach the meadow and look down through the glen. Even from such a distance, the Black Cottage looms large beneath the shade of tall oaks. The yard, wild with growth— seeded grasses and flowers—is bordered on the east by a broad stream, which finds its source deep beneath the rock of Mount Horn. The cottage itself is not actually black but brown brick with white wood and dark brown timbering. In the warmth of the May day, no smoke rises from any of the chimneys atop its gabled roofs, Jules gazes at it in wonder. It is not what she imagined, but it is grand. And then Caragh stops short and puts her down in the grass.

Two small crowds stand in the meadow, all dressed in black. One is led by a tall, imposing woman with white blond hair pulled back into a tight bun. Their faces seem frozen into stern expressions, heads tilted slightly back. The other is led by a woman in a soft, flowing cloak, with bright blue gemstones sewn into the hem. Later, Jules will remember nothing else about her, aside from those gemstones and the nervous way she clasped her hands.

"Milones," an older woman says to Caragh and Jules. She is thick around the middle and through the legs, her dark blond hair turned stiff with gray. "You are late."

"We are late, but we are here, Midwife," Caragh replies, and Jules tugs on her arm. Surely Caragh should not speak so to the woman presiding over the ceremony. "Though I'm sorry if we kept you."

"We can't be that late," says Matthew. "Wasn't that light show the Westwoods just arriving?"

The old woman looks at Matthew sternly, and Jules thinks he must be very stupid. Even she can see that the lightning must have come from the tall little girl with black hair and eyes, holding on to her sisters, a storm cloud and sweat across her brow.

They are the queens. Jules thinks she ought to bow, but she cannot stop staring. The three little girls are all alike in coloring, with black hair and eyes, but otherwise, they are each different, no two the same height or with similar features. They are nearly Jules's very same age, though they seem older, even as the smaller two weep fiercely.

"That's enough, Mirabella," the Midwife says.

The girl in the center of the triangle shakes her head. Her black tresses blow across her cheeks and tiny shoulders.

"No," she cries. "They are afraid, Willa!"

"That one is ours," says the matriarch of the Westwoods. She cocks a smile at the Arrons, gathered at the adjacent edge.

"Clearly," the tall Arron woman replies. "Sparking storms and misbehaving. Emotional and unreliable, as so many elementals are."

Every proud Arron face wears a frown so deep they look like scars. *They are a pale family,* Jules thinks, though she has heard others describe their beauty as "icy." After three poisoner queens, they are the strongest family on the island, and the richest. Joseph once told Jules that they had become so strong, even their blood had turned to poison, but Grandma Cait and Grandpa Ellis said those were only wild tales. In the old days, they said, a poisoner's blood could turn toxic, but only a queen's. And even then, it was rare. *How do they know?* Jules asked, wondering whose job it was to taste the queen's blood, and her grandma Cait had made Ellis stop teasing.

In the middle of the meadow, the three queens listen to the insults spoken between their new families with wide, frightened eyes.

"My Goddess," Aunt Caragh murmurs. "They weren't prepared for this. Look at them. They are only children."

"Poisoner Queen Katharine," the Arron matriarch says. She holds out her hand for the girl to come, but the queens only huddle closer together, so she sighs and snaps her fingers. "Willa. What kind of spoiled girls have you raised? Separate them. Now."

The Midwife stares into the grass. She seems so tired, and sad, and Jules wishes the girls would not be taken away. That Willa would not be left alone again inside the Black Cottage, alone until the next generation of queens is born. It is a great honor for a priestess to serve as Midwife, but to Jules it seems very hard.

"Come along now, Queen Mirabella," Willa says. "Let them go." She does not look at the little queens when she says this, but they look at her, all betrayal and tears.

"Let me go with them," Queen Mirabella begs. "Just to get them settled!" She grips her sisters tightly, and the Arron woman clears her throat.

"Oh, do it yourself, Natalia," Willa snaps.

Natalia Arron strides forward on long legs. Her blond hair is tied back in a bun so tight that the elemental wind cannot touch it. To Jules she seems ageless, too strong and beautiful to be old, too hardened and commanding to be young. Jules watches in wonder as little Mirabella raises her chin and stares her down.

"You will protect her," she says as she holds her sisters tight.

"And treat her like a precious stone?"

The look on Natalia's face says she would very much like to slap the girl, but she does not. Mirabella is a queen. Instead, Natalia shouts, "Westwoods!"

And the Westwoods come forth. Such is the clout of the Arrons after so many years of ruling the Black Council. The Westwoods grasp Mirabella by her thin arms and pull, and the younger queens start to scream, reaching for their sister only to have their hands slapped away. Jules hides half her face in Caragh's blowing skirt as Mirabella rages. The wind rises, loud enough to cover the Westwoods' words of comfort, but not enough to mask the queens' cries.

Soon, Mirabella is gone, dragged into the trees of the Greenwood, and the storm goes with her. In the meadow, two little queens stand together, chest to chest, wrists locked behind each other's backs.

"Caragh," Jules whispers, and tugs on her arm.

"Shush, Jules. Wait our turn."

But Jules cannot watch them be pulled apart again. And she knows the name of the queen they have come for. Arsinoe. Arsinoe the naturalist, who will be hers to take care of, and Joseph's too, whether he likes it or not. So she pulls free of her aunt, and steps into the meadow.

"Queen Arsinoe?" she asks, and holds out her hand.

The queens' heads raise from each other's shoulders. The taller of the two looks at her, and Jules knows she is Arsinoe. Jules smiles. She points to herself and then to her aunt and Matthew.

"I'm Jules Milone. This is my aunt Caragh and our friend Matthew. We've come to take you back to Wolf Spring."

Arsinoe's cheeks are streaked with tears and dirt. She looks at Jules, and Jules holds out her hand again. Then the queen looks back at her smaller sister and whispers to her.

"No!" the littler girl says. "They are mean!"

"You have to go, Kat," Arsinoe says. "And be good. We will see you again."

For the first time, Natalia Arron acknowledges Caragh, Matthew, and Juillenne. Her eyes slide over them only for a moment, but Jules dislikes the way the look feels, and stands up straighter.

"Good," Natalia says, and takes the littlest queen's arm. "Come, then." She stalks away, nearly too fast for the girl to keep up, dragging Katharine along as she stares back over her shoulder.

Suddenly, Katharine pulls back hard.

"Arsinoe!" she shouts, and Arsinoe springs forward like a cat. She scratches wildly at Natalia Arron's arms and face, drawing blood before Willa can pry her off. When Arsinoe's arms are held fast, Natalia slaps her across the face.

Caragh and Matthew gasp, and in Jules's stomach, butterflies fight with wasps, afraid and outraged.

"You do not strike a queen," Willa growls.

"That one is no queen crowned," Natalia says. "That one is walking dead." She pulls Katharine, crying, out of the meadow, and the Arron procession follows into the trees.

"Come on, Caragh Milone," says Willa, and softly strokes

Arsinoe's wild black hair, stuck down with sweat and snot and tears. She kisses the girl once and then turns away, back down the meadow toward the cottage. She has raised the queens from birth. And now her work is finished.

Arsinoe stands by herself. A queen should not look so sad or lost or beaten. Jules walks closer, and when Arsinoe does not move, she takes one more step and folds the other girl in her arms.

ROLANTH

The journey from the Black Cottage to Westwood House marks the most miserable days of Mirabella's life. She is ill with the memory of her last moments with Arsinoe and Katharine. She hears the echoes of their cries and feels the ghosts of their fingers grasping at the sleeves of her dress. As for her new family, they have barely spoken to her. "Sit her up straight," the matriarch, Sara Westwood, said. "Get the queen some water." Never "Mirabella." Never by her name, or to her, at all.

When she finally stopped screaming, after several long minutes in the carriage, they were relieved. They wiped her dry and patted her all over, as if she were a horse. Not one of them has dared to look her in the eye.

"Not long now until we reach Rolanth," Sara Westwood says to her brother, Miles.

"Should we stop and send a rider ahead?" he asks. "So the

people can turn out to greet her?"

Sara glances in Mirabella's direction. "I am not sure. After what happened at the claiming, and in front of the Arrons—"

"At least they can have no doubts about what she can do," says Miles. "The strength of her gift."

"Still . . . perhaps we had best wait until she is settled at home. Bree will calm her in no time—you will see. Then she can face the crowds."

"I would not mind," Mirabella says softly. "I would like to meet people."

Sara and Miles look at her, finally. So do the two quiet, frightened Westwood girls. Cousins, she has gathered, who are visiting only for the prestige of the claiming and will not stay and reside with them at Westwood House.

Mirabella tries to smile. Perhaps it does not look queenly enough, because Sara huffs and turns to look out the window. These people are flighty as birds. Why are they not like Willa? Why do they not seem to know what to do?

At the Black Cottage, Willa schooled all the queens, teaching them how to read and write, showing them numbers and arithmetic. And when Katharine fell asleep atop an open book, and Arsinoe wandered outside to chase the chickens around, she would teach Mirabella about the elemental city of Rolanth. Now Mirabella yearns to see it outside of the artists' renderings. To see the river rush out to the sea and to walk beside it through the Central District, where it is slowed to a crawl by locks and barges. She has imagined the smell of the evergreens and the ocean salt, and the sound of her heels against the stone of Shannon's Blackway, high on the basalt cliffs near Rolanth Temple. But it seems she will not even be permitted to look out the window.

She tries to catch Sara's attention again, to show her that she is a queen, that she has been raised as one and knows how to behave. At the cottage, with her sisters, Mirabella never felt small, and as the oldest, she never felt young. But she feels both very small and very young in the carriage full of Westwoods. Finally, after a long time of silence, she falls asleep, curled up into the seat with her legs tucked into her skirt.

"Queen Mirabella."

She wakes to a hand on her shoulder.

"You slept a long time. We are here. Home, at Westwood House."

Mirabella opens her eyes. They have been many days in the carriage and only stopped to change horses, never to sleep in a proper bed. In between griping about the Arrons, Sara had muttered about the preciousness of the queen and how important it was to get her back to Rolanth quickly. But as Mirabella steps out of the carriage on wobbly legs, she does not feel like a queen at all. Only dirty and hungry and faintly ashamed.

She looks up, blinking in the bright light, at Westwood House. It is indeed a grand place, at least twice the size of the Black Cottage. The carriage is stopped before the front steps, parked on a stone-paved drive that circles a tall, gurgling fountain.

"You are most welcome here, Queen Mirabella," Sara says, seemingly more at ease now within the confines of her property, high in the hills above the city proper and surrounded by evergreens.

"It is red," says Mirabella, and Sara raises her eyebrows.

"Ah. Yes. Old red brick. Perhaps you expected the limestone white and marble of the rest of the city."

She had not known what to expect. She moves off the drive and up the walk to the house, where the small staff of servants stands assembled to greet her. On the end, a little girl about Mirabella's age is straining against the hand of one of the maids. She wriggles with silent ferocity until she pulls free and races to stop before Mirabella and Sara.

The girl is so excited she is about to burst, yanking on the ends of her bright brown braids.

"Mother," she groans finally. "Introduce me!"

"Queen Mirabella, this is my daughter, Bree."

Bree reaches out immediately and takes Mirabella's hands.

"I am going to be your foster sister," she says. "Our rooms are very close. On the same floor. I always wanted Mother to have more babies, but so far she has not, but I am so excited you are here!"

"Give the queen some room to breathe," Sara says, and Bree quiets. She does not let go of Mirabella's hands, only drops one and moves to the side. Mirabella tries to listen as they take her through the vast house, and Bree is kind, and it is nice to be looked at again and called by her name. But when they finally leave her alone in her new, richly furnished bedroom, she sinks down beside the bed and hugs her knees. Bree wants to be a good foster sister, but she is no replacement for Arsinoe and Katharine.

"Be brave," she says to herself. "Do not cry."

For many weeks afterward, Mirabella does her best to appear cheerful and to be good and dutiful, for Willa has taught her that being a queen is about serving as much as it is about ruling. She goes where she is told to go and wears what she is told to wear. She compliments the Westwoods' household, their cooks, their city, and their fashion sense. She keeps her own room tidy and tries to help Bree to tidy hers (though that may truly be a lost cause) and impresses Sara with her grasp of the estate accounts.

For a while it seems that all will go as planned. The Westwoods are pleased, and parade her about Rolanth like a new and prized horse. She makes appearances at the best stalls in Penman Market and at the best shops in the high street. She prays to the Goddess every evening before the altar in Rolanth Temple. And everywhere she goes, the people of the city gawk. They stare and they whisper, and the bravest of them touch her clothes: the edge of her sleeve or the hem of her skirt. They ask questions about her, but never of her: "Is it true that her gift came when she could barely walk?" "Is it true that she has command of all the elements? And even the weather?" "I heard rumor that she has a temper, but she seems perfectly sweet and docile. . . . What chance does a docile queen have, even with a gift as strong as hers?"

Always, Sara answers for her with confidence, though Mirabella does not understand why they are shocked that she is strong or why her chances must be good. She wonders about it, but does not worry, for Sara seems to wave it off, and it must be something far away.

For a time, it seems that it may all be well, until one afternoon when Mirabella and Bree sneak into Sara's sitting room to surprise her with some raspberry cake.

The girls steal into the room like thieves, each holding one side of a silver tray. They duck down behind the arm of the sofa, and Bree presses her lips tightly together to stifle a giggle. The cake is not much to look at, but they iced it themselves with swirls of raspberry frosting, and the taste is very good; not too dry and not too sweet. Sara will like it. She will press her palms to her cheeks and close her eyes on the first bite. Then she will gather Bree and Mirabella in her arms so they can help her eat the rest.

They bring her so many surprises like this that Mirabella wonders how she can still be so surprised every time.

"It is a long time until the Ascension," Sara says to Uncle Miles, who is seated across from her in the green chair. Sara's sitting room is full of the swirling blues and blue-greens that she favors, and often being in it feels to Mirabella like being underwater. It is a calming room. An elegant space. And she and Bree are mischievous dolphins.

"Already the city loves her," says Miles. "There are so many offerings now at the temple. So many lit candles. She will have all the support she needs. We do not need the Black Council. And we do not need to fear the Arrons."

"We all need to fear the Arrons. Westwoods, elementals, down to the last—we ought to fear them. They are too strong now and dug in like ticks. We have the chosen queen, but they will not give way easily. I would not be surprised if it costs more than queensblood to place Mirabella on the throne."

The smiles fade from Bree's and Mirabella's faces. They have come at a bad time. Sara's voice is unhappy and serious, and Uncle Miles is not his usual lighthearted self.

"Whatever the cost," says Miles, "it will be worth it. The poisoners have had their way for too long. Choked us with taxation and mainland tariffs. Rolanth was the jewel of the island in Grandmother's time. And when she fought their injustices, they put her in a cell. Poisoned her in the dark with one of their concoctions."

"I have not forgotten, Miles."

"No one has. But it will stop now. Queen Arsinoe and Queen Katharine . . ."

Mirabella freezes at the mention of her sisters' names.

"They are weak. Mirabella will kill them easily. Quickly. Certainly faster than any of these poisoner queens have managed to kill their sisters."

Mirabella looks at Bree. Bree's eyes are wide, but out of fear, not of surprise. Mirabella's world tilts as she half listens to Sara going on about unclear oracles and quick deaths, death by lightning bolt or death by fire. Kill Arsinoe and Katharine. It is so terrible that she almost laughs. She must have misheard. How could anyone ever think to kill Arsinoe and Katharine? How could anyone ever think that *she* would?

The tray of raspberry cake clatters to the floor, the icing smearing across the deep blue rug like sea foam. Sara and Uncle Miles leap to their feet.

"Queen Mirabella! Bree!" Sara glares at her daughter. "What in the world are you doing?"

"We brought you cake," Bree answers, and begins to cry.

Neither adult moves to comfort her. They stare at Mirabella, afraid.

"You want me to kill my sisters?" she asks, and neither replies. Bree cries harder. Bree is a child. A little girl. But though they are the same age, Mirabella is no child. She is a queen. An eldest triplet.

"Mirabella," Uncle Miles says. "Why worry about such dull, grown-up business? And now we have frightened you and ruined this sweet surprise."

"No. What you were saying before," Mirabella says, undeterred. "A queen is to kill her sisters?"

"Mirabella—"

"Tell me!" When Mirabella shouts, a crack of lightning rattles the house, and even Sara flinches.

"You should not have heard this," Sara says. "There is plenty of time for such difficult things when you are older."

"But it is true," says Mirabella, and outside the rain starts.

It pelts the roof and the sides of the house, harder and harder, turning to hail, and thunder booms against the cliffs of the Blackway, growing louder until Bree covers her ears.

Sara reaches for the queen, but Mirabella screams and sends the flames in the candles high, scorching the walls. "Miles! Bree! Put them out!"

Little Bree is too afraid to move, but Miles clenches his teeth, pitting his gift against the queen's. He is older, and more practiced, and the candles snuff to smoke. But neither he nor Sara nor anyone else can stop the ferocity of the storm.

"Queen Mirabella, please!"

Shutters tear loose from the house. Windows rattle and threaten to shatter. Lightning strikes so close that the foundation shakes, and every elemental inside feels the electricity through the bottoms of their feet.

"I will not!" Mirabella screeches. "I will never, I will never, I will n—"

The storm eases when she falls to the floor, after Miles leaped behind her and used a heavy lamp to strike her on the back of the head.

GREAVESDRAKE MANOR

❧

Queen Katharine walks through the hallways of Greavesdrake Manor, holding tight to the seam of Edmund the butler's pant leg. The great house that the Arron family occupies is easy to get lost in and makes Katharine feel even smaller than she already is. Last week in the library she had to fight her way out of the folds of a curtain. And the ballroom is so large that the entire Black Cottage could fit inside.

As they go down the halls, their footsteps echo, and Katharine keeps glancing behind them, sure that Miss Genevieve is lurking about, ready to jump out and frighten her. The game was funny at first, but grows less so due to its frequency, and Miss Genevieve pinches hard enough to leave marks.

"There is no one back there, little queen," Edmund says. He looks down and winks at her over the top of his silver tray. "Miss Genevieve is already in the courtyard with the others. They have been playing croquet."

"She must like that game very much," says Katharine. "Since it lets her use such a big mallet."

Edmund chuckles, and she giggles back, though she does not know what is funny. Genevieve would like things with big mallets. She seems to like anything that allows her to hit.

They wind through the rear kitchens and step outside to make their way to the courtyard. The Arrons had erected black-and-white tents; more shade for visiting family than the alder trees could provide. Edmund leads her to the largest tent, where Natalia sits, watching her sister, Genevieve, and brother, Antonin, play a round with the younger cousins.

"There you are," she says as Katharine enters. Edmund places the silver tray down onto the table, and Katharine curtsies to Natalia and sits on the chair opposite. "And you have brought the May wine. How lovely."

"May wine," says Katharine. "Is it called that because of the month? Are we only to drink it in May?"

"May wine is a poisoner tradition." Natalia takes hold of the clear pitcher, full with bright, golden liquid. "We drink it always, but it is especially for the children. Let me show you."

She pours the wine into a silver cup and holds it out for Katharine to sniff. The scent is acidic and sweet, slightly grassy. Katharine wrinkles her nose.

"The toxin is from the woodruff plant," Natalia explains. "But it is not too much. That is why even those early in their gift are safe to drink it. Like children. And also because it is best served like so." She takes up a set of tongs and drops three lumps of sugar into the cup. She pauses, raises an eyebrow at the queen, and then drops in a fourth, making her giggle. "Almost done," Natalia says, but first she takes a large strawberry and makes fast slices into the tip, then uses her fingers to spread the fruit like a fan. She dips the berry into a bowl of honey and then drops the whole sticky mess into the cup of wine.

Katharine holds the cup in both hands and sips as Natalia licks her fingers. She can still smell the grassy bitterness, but the drink is sweet and wonderful.

"Well? What do you think?"

"It is delicious," Katharine says, and takes another sip. Natalia smiles and goes back to watching the cousins at their game. To Katharine's eyes, no woman in the world could be more beautiful than Natalia Arron. Her blond hair blazes like sunlight, and her lips are as red as summer apples. Everything about her is regal and elegant. Every step she takes is sure. The other Arrons, and the servants, are more than a little afraid of her, but since Katharine arrived at Greavesdrake, Natalia has been nothing but kind.

Katharine sips her drink and watches the croquet balls tumble across the lawn. No one asks her to play. No one pays her much mind at all, except to glance at her occasionally with curious looks on their faces. But that is fine with Katharine. The day is sunny and pleasant, and the May wine is cool in her belly. She has never cared for croquet anyhow; Arsinoe would never follow the rules when they tried to play at the cottage, and the mallets are too tall for her to swing comfortably.

After some time, Natalia stands and calls to Genevieve.

"I am going inside to settle some accounts," she says to her sister. "And then into the capital. I will not return until suppertime. Can you play the hostess until then?"

"Of course, sister," Genevieve replies, her mallet resting against her shoulder, and her pretty, lilac eyes sparkling.

"Serve more May wine to the children. It is weak enough for them. But do not taint it with anything else. The littler cousins have no gift at all yet, and we do not want there to be vomit in the grass."

It is on her third glass of May wine that Katharine's stomach starts to hurt. At first, she tries to conceal it, thinking that the pains will pass, like the time that she and Arsinoe ate all of Willa's plum tart and could not walk for hours. But then her head begins to throb, and her vision darkens. She is vaguely aware that she is throwing up, just as her body thumps against the soft, green grass beneath the black-and-white tent.

When she wakes later she is nauseous and shivering, but at least she is in her bed inside the manor and no longer stretched out on the lawn for everyone to see. She half opens her eyes in the candlelight. It is dark. Nighttime. Of the same day? She hopes so.

Natalia and Genevieve stand just outside of her bedchamber, in her sitting room. Their voices are hushed but angry. Perhaps frightened. She moans, so they will know they do not need to be quiet, and so they might come in and see her. Their talking pauses, but they remain outside.

Curious and a little more awake, Katharine rolls and looks through the doorway. Just the sight of Natalia calms her: back straight, wearing a dove gray shirt with the sleeves rolled to the elbows. The front of her black trousers are messed, and Katharine realizes with horror that she must have thrown up on her.

"She is weaker than Camille ever was, and now the whole family knows it," Genevieve hisses.

"And whose fault is that? How many cups of May wine did she have? Did I not tell you to watch her? To mix the wine weak? Now we have a sick queen and two sickening cousins in a carriage back to Prynn."

"This story will spread. The people will dive upon it. Especially with the tales coming out of Rolanth about the elemental queen. How strong she is. The storms she produces. Queen Mirabella—"

There is the sound of a slap, and Genevieve cries out.

"How many times must I say not to speak their names? Nowhere that she might overhear."

"She is unconscious," Genevieve says.

"I do not care. No one speaks their names. They do not exist. A queen's memory is short at this age, and in a year or two, she will have forgotten them entirely, as long as we do not help her to remember. Ignore her when she asks of them, as if you had not heard. And never speak the names!"

Clothing rustles, and Genevieve squeaks again. Even

disoriented and sick, the sounds frighten Katharine, and she huddles down into her blankets.

"We will have an easier time of it, once she forgets," says Natalia.

"We will have an easier time of it once her gift strengthens," says Genevieve. "Let me train her. Let me coax it out. Such methods have worked before, and even if the gift is slow to show, at least she will build natural tolerances."

A long pause, and Katharine raises her head to find Natalia staring in at her. Katharine sinks back on her pillows and feels safe. Natalia will not leave her. She will probably stay by her bed all night. Her eyes drift shut. Nothing bad can happen as long as Natalia is there.

WOLF SPRING

--- ❧ ---

*T*he house of the naturalist Milone family rests on the outskirts of the village of Wolf Spring. It is an agrarian land, some residents with more of a gift than others, but the strongest magic in the region bears a naturalist slant. Crops and livestock grow well, and fish are plentiful in the waters outside Sealhead Cove, named not for its shape but for the propensity of seals to bob up and down in the waves.

Joseph's family lives on the cove. His father builds ships and occasionally sails them, though most of his crafts run along the coast to the richer families of Prynn and Beckett. Neither he nor the three Sandrin sons have any gift, though Matthew insists he can charm the fish and dolphins like his mother, and Joseph claims to have the sight. Little Jonah is not likely to show a gift either, though he is only a toddler and it is too early to say.

Juillenne and Joseph bob in the water alongside the seals

in the warm waves. From the tip of the dock, the landmass of the island stretches out in both directions. Fennbirn Island. Called so by the outsiders who find their way across the sea and through the mists. To its inhabitants, it is only the island, and Grandpa Ellis says that its true name is guarded on the tongues of the eldest women. They bite down on it, angry that the young cannot even pronounce it, let alone understand what it means. Their anger will swallow the word whole, and in a generation or two, the island's true name will be forgotten entirely.

Juillenne doubts that the island cares, one way or the other, what it is called. To her it is only home, vast and unending, dotted with mountains and inland lakes, streams and cities of varied people of varied gifts. Caragh says that Jules's mother, Madrigal, ran away from the island for bigger things. But Jules does not understand how anyone could want something more than the island and its Goddess.

On the dock, nearer to shore, Caragh sits with Matthew, with their legs dangling in the water, pant legs rolled to their knees. Beneath the surface, Joseph tugs on one of Jules's ankles, and she tries very hard to keep from kicking him in the face.

He comes up and spits water.

"Race you to the dock," he says. Jules shakes her head. She is in no mood to be beaten today. Today she would wish she had a shark for her familiar, to drag Joseph under and give her time to pass, and she has heard a hundred times from the old folk of Wolf Spring that such wishes are dangerous, for the Goddess might grant them true.

Jules presses her finger to her lips and nods toward Matthew and Caragh, ripe for splashing. She and Joseph skim side by side through the cove, smooth and silent as water striders. Then they hang off the dock wood and wait for their moment.

"Is that what it's like every time, do you think?" asks Matthew. "The lightning. The crying. Pulling them apart. I know I said so to Jules, but I really did think that was only a story."

"I don't know," Caragh replies. "Goddess willing, it will be the only claiming we ever have to see."

"Maybe it was the Midwife's fault. Maybe she didn't prepare them right."

"How do you prepare a child for something like this? How will we prepare her now? Queen Arsinoe's been with us a week, and all she does is stare out toward Rolanth. In case her sister sends up a bolt." Caragh nods down the dock, where Arsinoe stands scanning the sky.

"Let her have those lightning bolts. Because one day they'll stop. Then Arsinoe won't see her lightning again until the Ascension, and it will be for a totally different reason."

Jules grasps Joseph's shoulder, and he looks at her, brows creased. She pulls them both under the cover of the dock.

"Three dark sisters, all fair to be seen," says Matthew.

"The way it's always been," says Caragh. "And it never seemed cruel until I saw it firsthand."

"It isn't cruel. It's in their nature. Always three, always in December, conceived at Beltane, always daughters. A queen isn't like us. They aren't normal people with normal gifts. It's just how it is."

"Not always," Caragh whispers. "Sometimes there is a fourth. A Blue Queen. Do you remember the year of the birth? Some of the oracles spoke of that. They thought the lack of omens meant something special."

Matthew throws something into the water. It splashes beside Joseph, and he and Jules retreat farther along the dock.

"Something special," Matthew mocks. "Now the lack of omens is an omen in itself?"

Caragh's expression is distracted, lost in some memory. Then she shakes her head, hard. "You're right. It's foolish. Omens and oracles. Means nothing."

"It would have been better if it had. But there hasn't been a Blue Queen since . . ."

"Queen Illiann," says Caragh. "Born ten generations of queens ago. Reigned in harmony until the birth of her triplets forty-six years later. A long reign. I asked Dad."

"What's a Blue Queen?"

Arsinoe's low voice is a surprise to all. Jules had not heard her footsteps even from underneath the wood.

"Nothing," Caragh answers quickly. "Only a very lucky and rare queen."

"Only one of my sisters or I will be the real queen," says Arsinoe. "So if she is so lucky, is it always her?"

"Yes."

"Then what happens to her sisters?"

Above the wood, Caragh clears her throat. "Why don't you go into the market? The catch should be cleaned and the stalls frying them up for sandwiches by now."

Arsinoe says nothing. She walks away, back down the dock, and Jules and Joseph swim along in her shadow. By the time she stops, they are in such shallow water that they can almost touch the bottom.

She is so sad, Jules thinks, and Joseph frowns, as if he can read her mind. He takes a breath and dives down with a great splash, loud enough that Arsinoe must know they are there, so Jules swims out a few strokes and smiles at her, squinting into the sun.

It has been strange, sharing the house with the sullen, black-haired little girl. She spends most of her time staring out the window for Mirabella's lightning, or whispering Katharine's name over and over under her breath, like a spell they do not know. But she eats (a lot), and she sleeps, and she is always polite. And to think that Jules feared the young queen would be constantly underfoot, hanging on her sleeve and getting in the way of her and Joseph's fun.

Joseph surfaces and surges up and out onto land like a seal, grabbing the dock and rolling onto the wood beside Arsinoe without much grace. Still, he does it in one try. It takes Jules a lot longer, scrambling and huffing. Then they sit on either side of Arsinoe, and Joseph spreads out the things he has carried up from the bottom of the cove: three curved shells, black and white and speckled brown. He taps the shell in the middle, and a hermit crab's legs poke out of its oversize home. He prods it again, and it waves its tiny antennae.

Jules taps one of the other shells, and the crab inside scuttles back. Joseph pulls Arsinoe to her knee. It takes a moment, but finally she gets curious enough to tap the last crab. For the next few minutes at least, her sister's lightning is forgotten as the three children prod their crabs to see whose will be first to make it back into the water.

Six weeks after the Milones took the young queen into their house, Caragh lies on her back in the meadow beside Dogwood Pond, with her head on Matthew Sandrin's stomach. Her familiar, Juniper, rests her brown snout in the crook of her arm, the hound's back covered with yellow and white wildflower petals that Matthew shook over them both. The day is warm and lazy, and Caragh traces patterns along Matthew's forearm, wrapped around her chest. It is not often that she gets a day to herself. Usually, she is too busy raising her younger sister's daughter.

Jules is Madrigal's child, but it has been years since Caragh has thought of her as anything but her own. Caragh watches her every day as she walks through the flowers and vegetables in the garden, coaxing their stalks and stems to grow up straight, urging their roots to run deep. She sees her love for the island, and for the Goddess who runs like water through the heart of it all. Jules is hers. The Goddess's and Caragh's. Jules is nothing like Madrigal.

"What are you thinking about?" Matthew asks.

"Nothing."

He smiles, that rakish smile that Caragh worries will

someday get Juillenne into the same kind of trouble with Joseph that she is in with Matthew.

"Nothing," he repeats, and pulls her farther into his arms. "Liar."

Caragh kisses him, pressed against his chest, and it is not long before Matthew's hands change from gentle to searching. Juniper growls and grabs Matthew's shirt, but before she stalks off, she licks his hand. Juniper is Caragh's familiar, and because Caragh loves Matthew, so does she.

"Caragh Milone," he says against her lips, and again as he kisses her neck, as she arches to meet his hands, fumbling at the buttons of her shirt. "Marry me."

Caragh's heart pounds between them. She slips her arm around his back and holds him fast when she says no.

He is not surprised. He has asked before and heard the same. His hand slides down, along her leg, and she holds her breath.

Afterward, when they lie entwined, half dozing in the late-afternoon sun, he asks why she said no this time.

"Because you don't mean it," she says quietly. "You're only seventeen, Matt. And I have five years on you."

"I don't know why you keep telling me that. Like you think I haven't heard. Or can't count."

Caragh smiles. Matthew thinks their ages are just right. Strong-gifted naturalists live long lives, so she will be one hundred and he will be ninety-five, and they will die together in their bed, on the same day. Caragh touches his face.

"If you can count, then count to three. And ask again then."

"Three days?"

"Matthew."

"Three months'?"

She shakes her head.

"Three years, Caragh," he says, "is forever to wait."

"To you it is. And that's why I'm saying no."

Three Years Later

ROLANTH

❦

S ara Westwood sits across from the High Priestess of Fennbirn Island. They have met in secret at an inn in Trignor, a coastal town with a port that smells as much of the sheep from the farms in Waring as it does of fish, but Sara does not mind the smell. She has quietly begged for this meeting for years, and this is as near as they could come to midway between Sara's city of Rolanth and the High Priestess's quarters in Indrid Down Temple.

"More ale?" she asks, and snaps her fingers for the serving girl. She does not call the High Priestess by her title, as she has come dressed in simple white-and-black temple robes that any priestess might wear. She does not even call her "Luca," her name, which is known the island-over.

After the ale is poured, High Priestess Luca regards her with sharp blue eyes.

"How is everything in your household, Sara?"

"Lucky to be standing, truth be told," Sara replies. "Thank the Goddess for reinforced roofs. They are most resistant to being torn off."

Luca chuckles. "You are being dramatic."

"High Priestess, I am not. The stronger she became, the more difficult she was to control. We have"—she pauses, ashamed—"we have taken to keeping her shut up in the basement."

Inside, belowground and away from windows, Mirabella is manageable. But they have still had to brick over the fireplace. And the nailed-down shutters on the exterior of the windows are not fooling anyone.

"A queen? Locked up in a basement?"

"We are failing her. We were not prepared."

Sara takes a large swallow of ale. They will do better. The Westwoods' time is just beginning. The Arrons will fade, and the Westwoods will rise, building up their homes and the city until Rolanth rivals the capital city of Indrid Down. If only they can shepherd this queen.

"There have been rumors," says Luca. "They say that she is a handful. But surely your letters were an exaggeration."

"I am not in the habit of exaggerating. And certainly not to you. She has not forgotten her sisters."

"A queen always forgets. Give her time."

Luca's voice is soothing but dismissive. She will seek to put Sara's mind at ease and leave her with no more than a pat on the head, if Sara lets her. And Sara has written too many letters, and pleaded with too many interim priestesses, for that.

"The people wished for an elemental queen," she says, her voice bitter. "They feared that there was nothing left to the Goddess but poisoners. And now that they have an elemental, they whisper that she is a handful. She is more than a handful. And we will fail if someone does not help us."

"At first, the strong queens are always difficult."

"It has been three years."

Luca takes a long drink of her ale and crunches through a baked, salted cracker. "How is she other than that? Does she look you in the eye? Respond to your emotions?"

"Yes. There are times when she is almost sweet." Sara knows what the priestess is asking. Madness in a queen is not to be borne, and would mean Mirabella's instant death. "She shows no sign of madness."

"The island can never have another Elsabet," Luca says, referring to Queen Elsabet, a sight-gifted queen who, upon foreseeing an assassination plot, had three whole houses of people executed without evidence.

"Never." Sara makes a pious gesture to the Goddess of the island. "But what do we do now? Is there anything that can be done?"

Luca grunts. "There is always something to be done. Fostering a queen is never easy. Did you think it would be? The temple must be neutral, Sara. I don't know what you would have of me."

Sara bows her head, and Luca sighs, as if she cannot take a moment more of Sara's pitiful face. "Do you really think she is a chosen queen? Our queens win their crowns through killing. People have their favorites, but if she truly is as strong as you say, her victory would be near assured."

"She is that strong. She is chosen. And she needs the temple to guide her. As all queens do. Surely you would go to the aid of any of the young queens in this way."

"Surely," Luca says.

Sara keeps her eyes on the table as the High Priestess mulls it over, weighing tradition against rightness, faith against action. But Sara knows that Luca hates the poisoners as much as she does. Though they may not have murdered Luca's grandmother, they have done even worse in wresting power away from the temple.

Luca wipes her mouth on a napkin and drops it beside her ale. "Well. You had better take me to meet the queen. Let us let her prove it."

When the door to the basement creaks open, Mirabella blinks curiously into the shaft of light. It is not the hour for lessons or feeding. Though it is difficult to tell in the darkness of her confines.

Bree's feet come slowly down the steps. She has even dared a small candle to light her way.

"Queen Mirabella," she says. "We are bringing you to meet someone very important today. Will you let me help you get dressed? We have prepared a bath, and a beautiful new gown, and I will style your hair if you like. . . ."

The stubborn part of Mirabella, that same part that grips on to memories of her sisters with slippery fingers, wants to flare Bree's candle up into her face. But the other part, that part that has rarely seen the sky in three long years, wins out. Besides, Bree's gift has shown with an affinity for fire. Maybe she is already strong enough to hold back the flare.

With a gentle touch, Bree leads her up the stairs, into the day. The light hurts at first, stinging her eyes. From the grimaces on the servants' faces, she must be hurting their eyes just as badly.

"Into the tub, Queen Mirabella."

They have dragged a deep copper tub into the center of the kitchen and filled it with hot, perfumed water. Two maids strip her of the filthy rag of a dress she wears until she stands in her underclothes, her limbs streaked with dust and her hair hanging in oily strings.

She steps into the tub and submerges immediately, the heat and weight of the water pressing down like a blanket. Water has always been her worst element. The most elusive. Almost playful in its propensity to ignore or disobey. But today is different. Today she can tell that it has missed her.

Mirabella surfaces and lets Bree and the maids wash her face and scrub her fingernails. It is nice to be touched. Nice to be warm. And after the bath, they wrap her in a soft dressing gown, and brush and brush the tangles out of her hair.

"Who is here?" she asks as they pull a dress of fine black wool over her head. "Who am I to meet?"

"No one is here," Bree replies. Over the last three years, Bree has grown lovely. Her chestnut hair is twisted into buns on the back of her head, and she wears a light blue skirt edged with black ribbon. "We must travel to meet them at Starfall Lake. You are to meet the High Priestess of the island. High Priestess Luca."

It takes a long time for High Priestess Luca and Sara Westwood to reach the end of the rocky, sloping path to the shores of Starfall Lake, but when they do, only Sara is out of breath.

"It surprises you." Luca stretches her arms. "You likely thought I would be old and soft. You have only seen me from afar, riding in fancy carriages and eating from silver platters on the festival days."

"I am impressed but not surprised. Have you ever been to the lake before?"

"Of course. Though not for several years. Starfall Lake. Named for the starfalls reflected in its waters, still commonly visible in the winter skies on this side of the island. It is lovely, is it not?"

"Yes, lovely," says Sara, her voice like a waving hand. The lake is not important. The only thing that is important is the small girl making her way around the shore opposite. Several Westwoods form a circle around her. It would look like protection had Luca not already heard about the queen's erratic behavior.

The Westwood party arrives and pays respect to the High

Priestess. Some wear temple insignia around their necks, and bow to her with unusual fervor, perhaps touched by the Goddess to become priestesses one day. Luca nods and lays distracted blessings upon their heads. Her focus is on the queen, as theirs should be, but the moment the Westwoods saw Luca, they flocked to her in relief and left Mirabella's side to hide behind the High Priestess's robes.

Queen Mirabella, meanwhile, has stepped into the lake up to her ankles.

"Mirabella," Sara Westwood says. "Will you come and meet the High Priestess?"

Other Westwoods begin to gather cautiously around the lake, closing in on the queen in a half circle, but Luca shakes her head. Mirabella walks closer, alone, and silly Sara feels the need to whisper, "Take care. She learns new tricks every day she is allowed outside."

Luca pays no mind. She slides out of her shoes and walks into the lake, up to her ankles in cool water on the warm, summer day, shoulder to shoulder with the queen.

"It is lovely here," she says.

"Yes."

"Nice. Quiet."

"Yes."

Mirabella is a queen of few words. Or perhaps she is only shy, like Queen Camille, and will chatter on and on if given the opportunity, in private. Luca looks her over quickly, from head to toe. A beautiful girl with even features and a firm set to her mouth, even at nine years old. Dark, determined eyes. She does not seem like the wild thing that Sara described, though that is perhaps because they have groomed and disguised her in thin black wool, and an airy veil.

"Do you know who I am?" Luca asks.

Queen Mirabella glances at her.

"You are the High Priestess. That much they have told me. But I know what a high priestess is. From my teachings. You are the leader of the temple."

"That is right. And who was your teacher?"

"The Westwoods teach me now. Sara and Uncle Miles. But my first teacher was . . . Willa."

"You remember her fondly?"

"I remember," Mirabella says, but Luca sees through her clenched teeth to the truth. The truth is that she remembers Willa, only not as well as she used to. And she remembers the other queens, though she remembers them even less so. The fight in her has become a fight against forgetting. That is where the anger stems from.

"It is all right to remember," says Luca. "You will not be punished for remembering."

"Why are you here?"

Luca cocks her head. She kicks a little, playfully, at the water of the lake.

"I go where the Goddess wills me." She smiles at the queen. "As we all must. As surely you do. Someone with a gift as strong as yours must feel her with every beat of your heart."

"The Goddess," Mirabella murmurs thoughtfully. "Willa said she was my . . . our mother."

"The Goddess is mother to us all. But to you, especially. You are her body, here, on the island. Her hand. As I am her ears and eyes. And her voice to the people."

"Why are you here?" Mirabella asks again, brow furrowing, and the lake shudders suddenly, the entire surface contracting, as if an earthquake struck someplace down deep.

"To meet you, of course. I am here because you are sad."

"What is that?" From the shore, Sara points down into the water. Luca cannot see what she means, but from the way everyone backs away, it cannot be good. "There's something in the lake!"

Mirabella draws the creature out of the water, and Luca gasps. The translucent, liquid body is oddly beautiful as it hovers above the surface. Perhaps it is the water spirit of Starfall Lake, given form. But if it is, then Mirabella can do something no elemental has been able to do in recent memory.

"I am not sad," Mirabella says, and Luca looks at her and sees dots of perspiration on the little girl's forehead. "I am angry."

"Queen Mirabella—"

"Give me back my sisters!"

The water creature dives onto Luca, stabbing watery fingers into her eyes and into her nose and ears. She hears the Westwoods screaming as the water forces its way down her throat. Luca wishes she could scream, but all she can do is flail, and fall to the ground, and get her arms wet as she tries to fight.

"Mirabella, stop!" Sara shouts. But the queen will not. There is steel in her spine, and ice in her heart that will not be melted by one dead priestess. But Luca knows that her murder will force them to say Mirabella is mad. The people will storm Indrid Down and demand she be put to death.

With a gargantuan effort, Luca wills herself to stop panicking. She looks at the queen with compassion. She holds out her hand. For a moment, she thinks it will not work, that the burning in her lungs will increase until her vision goes dark. But then the water splashes to the ground. She coughs it up until her throat is raw and her muscles sore, but she can breathe again.

The Westwoods circle around Mirabella, ready to drag her from the lake and lock her back where they found her.

"No!" Luca shouts in between her coughing. They back away, and Luca looks up at the queen fondly. "No one touches our chosen queen."

WOLF SPRING

———————— ❧ ————————

Arsinoe follows Jules as Joseph leads them on a merry chase through the woods. Try as he might, he cannot leave them behind. Both are still as slim-hipped as he is, and what Jules lacks in length of leg she makes up for in quickness. All three run for the sheer childhood delight of running and never seem to tire, though their cheeks are flushed red. It has been three years since Arsinoe joined them, and while she is still far more serious than Jules or Joseph, she will laugh now, and a mischievous, sarcastic edge has crept into her voice. She is happy. Jules and Joseph have become her friends, and if some part of her remembers that they are not to be replacements for others . . . Well, that part has fallen very quiet.

"Joseph, not so fast!" Arsinoe shouts from the back.

Joseph cackles and yells, "Faster!" He twists his head to look. She and Jules are right on his heels, and he smiles as though proud of them. Ahead, the path leaves the woods and broadens into the tall, sunlit grass of the meadow beside Dogwood Pond. Jules takes her chance, surging ahead of Arsinoe, short legs flying. She overtakes Joseph at the last moment and bursts through first, into the daylight.

"That's practically cheating!" Joseph says, and Arsinoe laughs. Her strides slow, and her muscles relax to weak-kneed slackness.

"She does it every time. You ought to know by now. You ought to expect it."

Arsinoe slaps Joseph on the back. But he does not reply or slap her in return like he usually does. He has stopped dead behind Jules, and both are staring at something across the field. Arsinoe blinks against the summer sun and puts a hand up to shield her eyes.

It is a young woman. A beautiful young woman in a vibrant green dress, and golden brown hair loose to her waist. Arsinoe thinks she knows this woman somehow, from somewhere, though she is certain she has never met her. And something about the way Jules is staring sets Arsinoe's teeth on edge.

Across the meadow, the woman holds out her arms and calls, "Juillenne!"

"Mother!" Jules shouts, and runs to her.

Caragh stands at the kitchen sink, scrubbing tender, fat carrots from her garden. This year, she and Jules have spent more time than ever in the fields coaxing crops, and the entire harvest is strong. Jules's gift has almost reached fullness. Ellis teases that when she is grown she will be able to feed Wolf Spring all by herself.

"Here, let me," says Caragh's mother, Cait, elbowing her way in. "You're too slow. Should be done already." Should have been done hours ago, while Caragh was out doing who-knows-what with that Sandrin boy, is what Cait means. But stolen hours with Matthew are worth all the snide comments that her mother wants to make. "Where's Juillenne?"

"Where she always is," says Caragh. "Playing with Joseph and Arsinoe."

"You should mind them. Nine is a mischievous age."

"So it is. And it goes too fast. They might as well have a bit of fun."

Cait scowls, a beautiful woman turned handsome by the years. She is tall, like all the Milone women save for Jules, and her bones are straight and strong.

"Is that what you're having with Matthew? A bit of fun?"

Caragh pours more water into the sink. "No. Matthew is different. Matthew, I intend to marry."

"Different," Cait says sadly. "Like it was for my aunt Phillippa. Like it was for my sister Rosaline."

Caragh squeezes the carrots almost hard enough to break them. Phillippa and Rosaline. She has heard those names so many times. Whispered in another room, or spoken right to her, as if she was them. Phillippa, who married Giuseppe Carlo. She threw herself off Hawthorne Bridge in the middle of winter, and her body cracked like a champagne flute against the

75

ice. Rosaline, who married no one but could not face the fertile womb of her sister Cait, and died alone in Portsmouth on the eastern coast.

The unlucky Milone sisters. The cursed ones who bore no children. No one knows where the curse came from. They only know that it is the curse of all Milones. Two girls are born each generation. And one is barren. Sasha and Phillippa. Cait and Rosaline. Madrigal and Caragh. And Madrigal has already had Juillenne.

"It's not the same for me," says Caragh.

"It's not," Cait agrees. "Because you're a Milone. A naturalist. And barrenness for us is"—she takes a quiet breath—"like tearing our hearts out."

"It's not the same for me *because I have Jules*," Caragh says. "I have Jules, and I'll be fine. Matthew loves her like she's his own." She does not say that she loves him. It is too much of an admission, and Caragh has always kept her feelings to herself.

"He's too young to be a father to Jules."

"He loves Jules," says Caragh, her voice far away.

"He is only a boy. He doesn't know what he loves." Cait scrubs the carrots hard, and Caragh knows that her mother is only saying these things because she is afraid to lose her to madness and solitude—or worse, to the ice beneath a winter bridge—when she has already lost one daughter to the mainland.

"You're so sure, are you?" Caragh jokes lightly. "Have a bit of the sight now, like little Joseph?"

"We all do on Fennbirn," says Cait. "We just blind ourselves to it when it suits us. When we need it most."

Caragh sighs. She starts to say more, but her mother has stopped listening. Cait stares out the window over the kitchen sink, into the yard and the garden that borders their long driveway.

"By the Goddess," Cait whispers, and dries her hands on a towel. She tears off her apron and throws it onto the countertop. "Ellis! Ellis, where are you?"

"What's wrong?" Caragh asks as Cait shoves past her and dashes into the yard. She follows to the door and looks out. If it is Jules, showing up again in head-to-toe mud, she will scrub the girl raw. But it is not Jules running up the drive to leap into Cait's arms.

It is Caragh's sister, Madrigal. It is Jules's mother.

No one leaves or is allowed to find the island if it is not by the will of the Goddess. That is what Caragh has always been taught. So she tries to accept it with a little bit of grace that her sister has returned. Surely the Goddess must have a purpose, beyond upsetting Caragh's carefully ordered and relatively happy life.

She watches through the window as her mother weeps and her father lifts Madrigal in a whirling embrace, like he used to do when she was a little girl. Madrigal, they cry. Madrigal is home.

For how long, and for what, Caragh wonders. No one has heard from Madrigal since she left the island six years ago to go to the mainland, and no one expected to. It is said that once a woman leaves Fennbirn, she begins to lose her memory. And then, slowly, her gift. Indeed, when Madrigal finally sees Caragh through the kitchen window, it is almost as if she does not recognize her.

"But I recognize you," Caragh whispers, and at her knee, Juniper growls. Whatever Madrigal has been up to on the mainland, it has only made her more beautiful. She is still slender, but rounded now in just the right places. Her light brown hair shines, and her eyes sparkle. Her familiar has already returned to her and perches on her shoulder: Aria, a pretty black crow. Madrigal cocks her head, and so does the bird.

"Caragh," she says in a tone that is somehow familiar and insulting. *Oh Caragh, there you are. Where else would you be?*

Caragh brushes her hands nervously against her skirt and goes to meet her sister at the front steps. Madrigal is dressed like an outsider, in a strangely cut dress of green silk. There are gold hoops in her ears, and gold bangles on her wrists. She holds on to Jules with one hand, and Jules holds on tight, as though afraid she will disappear if she lets go.

"I hope you don't mind that I didn't come straight here," Madrigal says. She wraps an arm about Jules's small shoulders. "I wanted to find my daughter first."

My daughter. The words swirl in Caragh's stomach like blood from a punch. She wonders whether on Fennbirn all sisters are meant to hate one another. Not only the queens.

"She has not grown tall." Madrigal cups Jules's face. "But

she has certainly changed since I saw her last."

"She was a baby when you saw her last," Caragh says, and Cait and Ellis look at her sharply.

"A baby." Madrigal smiles. "She was three and a half. Walking and talking and even slightly gifted. A baby. Caragh, what can you be thinking?"

Not far away in the grass, Arsinoe's pale face peeks out from behind Joseph. He seems curious, and confused, like he thinks he should be happy but cannot remember why. Arsinoe looks suspicious.

"Are you home for good, Mother?" Jules asks. "Home to stay?"

"I am, my Jules." Madrigal plants kiss after kiss into Jules's hair, and the family closes around them in a circle, all smiles and tears. No one sees Caragh press her fists into her middle, where it hurts so badly it must surely be bleeding.

GREAVESDRAKE MANOR

───────────── ⚜ ─────────────

*G*reavesdrake Manor rests at the western end of the capital city of Indrid Down and spills across woodland and meadow. The great house stands on a low central hill and has grown larger as the years passed, expanding steadily, as if the house has somehow learned to feed. One more poisoner queen, and Greavesdrake will spill over into the streets.

Its pitched roofs have been washed black, to show the Arrons' devotion to the crown. That is what Natalia told little Katharine that first day, more than three years ago, when the carriage drove up to it. But Katharine has come to believe that the roof is black for another reason: it screams down to the capital, and all across the island, *This is where your queens are raised.*

Katharine sits at her vanity table and lets her maid brush out her long black hair. Her eyes are hollow and haunted, and she is painfully thin. She has simply lost the taste for eating.

It is not easy to pretend to relish the poisoned food they serve. Nor to keep from crying when they put her to the scorpion's sting or lash the nettles across her back. But she tries. It is all part of being a poisoner queen. Natalia says it is her duty to become strong, her obligation—to the Arrons who house and clothe her and to the island that worships her like the Goddess. Take the pain into yourself, Natalia tells her, and you will grow strong.

But sometimes it feels like her gift will never be strong. Like it will never come, and she will never revel in the poisons like the Arrons do. It feels like she has been poisoned forever. She cannot even remember anything that came before.

"Shall we braid you, miss?" her maid asks, and Katharine does not reply. The maid will do it anyway.

A short while later, Katharine walks alone to the dining room for breakfast with Natalia. Her hair is done, and she has been fitted into a soft, fine dress of black muslin. When Natalia sees her, she smiles. Even drawn and miserable, Katharine is still very pretty, and all Natalia sees is a perfect poisoner queen.

"Good morning, Queen Katharine."

"Good morning." Someone pulls a chair out for her, and she sits in front of a bowl of oatmeal and a plate of cut strawberries.

"How are your studies?" Natalia looks severe as she always does, but not unkind. A red-and-black-striped coral snake is twisted around her wrist like a bracelet.

"Does it have a name?" Katharine asks.

"No." Natalia kisses it on the head. "But it is very beautiful.

Now. How are your studies? Is your new tutor more to your liking?"

"We are reading from *Toxicology: The Use of Poisons in Modern Medicine.*"

"Very good." Natalia lifts the silver off her own dish. She eats a soup for breakfast, a bitter broth steeped with poison mushrooms. For lunch she might enjoy blowfish or a salad of bloodroot. Dinner is meat tenderized and tainted with scorpion venom. Poison for every meal. Such is her strength.

Natalia promises that one day, Katharine will eat the same. But Katharine cannot imagine it.

"I have to go into the capital today, Queen Katharine. But I shall be back before supper."

Katharine puts down her spoon. "I would like to go with you," she says softly. "Perhaps . . . perhaps I ought to go with you, if I am to rule there one day."

During the short carriage ride to Indrid Down, Natalia studies Katharine as she looks out the window, nosed pressed to the glass like an excited puppy. At nine years old, she has little of the lanky, lithe quality that Queen Camille had. But then, queens do not pass down physical traits or talents. Nothing but the bloodline.

"Natalia," Katharine asks, "what are we going to do in the capital today?"

"We are going to the Volroy. Where *I* must meet with the Black Council. *You* will not meet with them until after you are crowned."

"Then what am I to do while I wait?" The little queen turns and blinks at her. There is no guile in her questions, no petulance. Only a genuine curiosity that awaits instruction. Katharine pulls a little bit at her sleeve, tugging the muslin down to cover the fading welt of a spider bite.

Natalia sighs. "Perhaps I can put off the council. I will show you the poison room. An entire room with a full inventory of poisons, both domestic and foreign. Common and rare. Curated by many Arrons before me, on expeditions to the mainland."

"An entire poison room? Is it larger than the one at Greavesdrake?"

"Not larger." The poison chamber at Greavesdrake is the size of a small ballroom. "But better stocked. I have added to its shelves myself, as did my brother Christophe, when he traveled through the mists to the exotic, tropical climes of the southern seas."

Queen Katharine leans forward, daydreaming of poison as she gazes through the window glass.

"A whole room of poisons, right in the Volroy castle. Is that because the queen is always a poisoner?"

"She is not always, and you know that." Natalia reaches out and taps her beneath her chin. "But our queens have kept this island safe for three generations, without war or intrusion. Our family has kept it safe. And if the Westwoods think they can do the same, with their breezes and rain clouds . . . Fennbirn needs a poisoner. It needs a queen to fear. Death and strength are the only true currencies on the mainland anymore."

The carriage halts at the gates and moves on when Natalia

nods to the guards. Inside the vast, chilled halls of the Volroy, eyes widen at the sight of the young queen, so rarely seen there.

"I should like to hang more tapestries when I am queen," Katharine remarks, quietly so her voice will not echo.

"And why is that?"

"So it will not feel so cold. Cold and distant and brittle. The Volroy was not made to be loved."

"Indeed it was not," Natalia replies. "It was made to endure." She leads the queen up the stairs of the East Tower, up and up and through the antechamber that leads to the room of poisons.

She steps in, and Katharine walks eagerly to the center of the stone floor. She marvels at the cabinets full of poisons, dried and liquefied and preserved, glittering malevolently in their vials. She reaches out to touch the long table of sealed wood, topped with glass, and Natalia grasps her by the wrist.

"Take care. Your gift has not come. You must wear gloves before you touch anything in this room. No matter how meticulously it is maintained, I will not take any chances with your tolerance."

She goes to a closet and selects a pair of small, lined gloves for Katharine to wear.

"Now," she says, and smiles, "shall we make something pretty? Something pretty, and something deadly."

The poison that they craft is called Winter's Blush, since it kills by constricting the blood vessels and making the body go cold all over. Sometimes the constriction causes the capillaries to burst as well, making the name even more fitting. It is a popular poison lesson for beginners, because it has only four ingredients and because of the pretty lilac color that it turns, and the way that it fizzes.

Katharine holds the stoppered vial gleefully between gloved fingers, admiring the purple hue. "It is like Miss Genevieve's eyes," she says.

Natalia chuckles. "She would love that you said that. But though it is beautiful, you must treat it with respect. As you must treat all poisons. A poison is not a plaything. It is sacred and serious business. As the head of the Black Council, I must concoct poisons to administer as punishment to those on the island who would do harm. Who commit crimes. Sometimes I must punish them to death. And as queen, you must do so as well."

The young queen slides the poison into the cuff of her sleeve, practicing her sleight of hand. She is still not very good at it. But she is no stranger to death and has heard such words before. Each time she turns a little less green.

"I will do what I must." Katharine looks at her in sudden alarm. "But you will be there with me?"

Natalia begins to clean the table, returning ingredient bottles to shelves and drawers, carefully brushing stray bits and dust into a bin to be destroyed. Queen Katharine may be small, and some, like Genevieve, may think her weak, but Natalia disagrees. She *is* small, and softhearted. She is kind. But she is also resilient and dutiful. She has never refused or hesitated in the face of poisoning. She will make a fine queen.

"Yes, Queen Katharine. I will always be with you." She wipes the blade of one of the short knives she used to cut a sliver of root and finds it so sharp that it sinks into her finger. She gasps as blood runs down her knuckle. "Foolish. Foolish and careless of me."

"Natalia, you are bleeding!" Katharine reaches for her hand and quickly wraps it in a clean cloth. She looks so concerned as she pats Natalia's fingers and squeezes them gently. And over such a small thing. "Is that better?"

"All better," says Natalia. And then she laughs and pulls the queen close. "You are such a strange girl, Kat. Such a strange and dear girl."

WOLF SPRING

Arsinoe and Joseph walk behind Jules and her mother by at least a dozen paces. They watch the pair suspiciously and wonder who this strange woman is, the strange woman with the beautiful face, whose very presence turns their friend Jules into an affectionate pet. Joseph pulls up a long bit of big bluestem out of the meadow grass and thwacks the other stalks as Aria the crow flaps overhead. She is never far from Jules's mother. Perhaps she is afraid of being left again.

Arsinoe tugs at the collar of her black shirt. She is the only one who has to wear black year-round, even in high summer, when it soaks up the sun and makes her so hot she might have a stroke.

"You should quit wearing black all the time," Joseph says, and he makes it sound so easy that she wants to hit him.

"Arsinoe!"

She looks up—they both do—and sees Madrigal waving

for them to come on. She is smiling, and the blades of grass move around her in a dance. She is hard to resist. Joseph runs at once, and after a moment, Arsinoe, the most skeptical and sullen queen born for at least the last thousand years, goes, too.

Madrigal grabs Arsinoe, and Arsinoe grabs Joseph, and Joseph grabs Jules, and they spin through the grass, churning up their own wind. Arsinoe and Joseph laugh, and Jules and Madrigal throw their heads back, and the butterflies come. All the butterflies it seems, from every crick and corner of Fennbirn. Monarchs, wood whites, orange tips, and black-and-yellow-striped swallowtails. They swirl into the meadow and fly over and under and around them. In the corner of Arsinoe's eye, flashes of blue and brighter yellow ignite in the grass: the wildflowers all blooming at once.

Finally, they fall apart onto their backs, laughing. Madrigal pulls fresh blooms of flowers to her nose, and Aria lands on her chest to eat a blue butterfly. Delicate wings cover Madrigal from head to toe, opening and closing in all colors. They are on Jules, too, but Jules does not seem to notice. She stares at her mother with such love it makes Arsinoe jealous, only she is not sure who she is jealous of.

"That was a very good game, Funny Eyes," Madrigal says. She reaches a finger out to touch her daughter's nose, and Jules's smile fades.

"I like your eyes, Jules," says Joseph. "I wish I had them."

"I didn't say I didn't like them," Madrigal says. "I only said they were funny. Which they are." She touches Jules's hair. "It's a pity though, that I didn't find a boy that Beltane with black, black hair. The butterflies look so pretty in Arsinoe's." She lets go of Juillenne and leans toward the queen.

"Do you feel the way they talk to you? Can you hear what they say through their beating wings?"

Arsinoe sits still a moment. She feels only their legs and furry antennae, tickling her scalp.

"No."

Madrigal sighs. She puts one hand on her crow and then tosses her into the air before she can eat any more butterflies. "I haven't been back on the island for two weeks, and already I've heard them whispering. 'Will she be strong enough to become the queen?' 'Could she be?' 'When will her gift start to show? She is already nine.'"

"I'm already a queen. That's why they call me Queen Arsinoe."

"But you aren't the only one. You know that, don't you?"

Jules and Joseph look at Madrigal, faces bleak, as if they sense she is about to ruin a sunny afternoon.

"Fennbirn has three queens in every generation," Madrigal goes on. "You don't just get the crown by virtue of being born. You have to fight for it." She prods Arsinoe in the belly playfully, and Arsinoe swats at her hand.

"I don't think I want to be crowned anyway."

Madrigal leans back with her elbows in the grass and clucks her tongue, like that is a very great shame. She brushes at the last of the butterflies lingering on her clothes—strange clothes from the mainland: tall leather boots with heels, and tight trousers.

"Caragh and Mum want to coddle you," she says. "Make you happy until your time comes. They want to treat you like a loser. Like you're dead already."

"Dead?" Jules sits up.

"That is what happens to the queens who lose. They are killed. But don't despair." Madrigal cups Jules's cheek with one hand and pinches Arsinoe's with the other. "There is plenty of time yet to train. To grow strong. To be the victor. And I am here now, and I will help you."

Caragh and Matthew walk the long dirt road that leads to the Milone house. It is a cool, pleasant walk thanks to the oaks that stretch their branches over the path, but still Matthew is quiet. He has been quiet all afternoon.

It is high and fading summer, as August draws toward close and minds turn toward the fall and the celebration of the Reaping Moon. It is a difficult time for naturalists, as their gift sings in anticipation of harvest but also shakes before the descending shadow of winter. In some it shakes so hard it feels like something trying to escape. For a barren Milone girl, it is a season to be driven mad as all across the island, pregnant Beltane bellies begin to show. Matthew knows this. Caragh suspects that he has always been aware of it, since he always seems aware of whatever she needs. How he knew she would need him that claiming day at the Black Cottage. How he knew that this turn of season was the first one to break her heart. In every other year, she had Jules.

The breeze moves the leaves overhead, and Aria the crow dives down on Juniper and caws loudly, making Juniper yip and scrunch her back. She tries to bite the bird out of the sky, but the crow is already up and out of danger. Caragh's heart sinks when she hears Madrigal's laugh, and sinks farther when she turns and sees Jules, Joseph, and Arsinoe walking up with her.

"Caragh Milone," Madrigal says. "What are you up to with this boy?"

"You should keep an eye on your crow," says Matthew, and Madrigal skips up to and around him. Her long brown hair flicks across his shoulder, and her fingers slide down his arms. Even when she is being a brat, she looks like a fairy. Twirls and sparkle. Gossamer wings.

"I always have an eye on my crow. Just like Caragh has on her *dog*." She taps Juniper's nose and looks back at Matthew. "I remember you. Matthew Sandrin. My how you've grown."

Caragh watches Matthew over her sister's shoulder. He stares at Madrigal like he hates her, but he still stares. Madrigal has always made everyone stare.

"Should we go home together?" Madrigal asks. "If you can keep up?" She spins away, and the children follow, as if pulled by an unseen leash. Jules does not even look at Caragh. None of them do. They are not their usual, rascal selves.

"Wait, Madrigal," Caragh says. "You children go on ahead. We'll catch up to you." The three of them walk on somberly, and Caragh senses a tension in them. A fear.

"What now?" Madrigal asks, and rolls her eyes.

"What did you do to them? Jules looks ready to wilt flowers."

"I didn't do anything to them. We called butterflies and grew grass. Arsinoe grew nothing. She won't last long, you know, if you keep treating her this way. She will be dead the moment the Quickening is over."

"You didn't speak to them of that?"

"Of course not."

"Madrigal, they are too young. She is not ready."

Madrigal crosses her arms. It has been more than two years since Arsinoe made any mention of her sisters. The memories have likely faded into nothing. But even if they have, she is still only a little girl. Too young a queen to start in with talk of the killing.

"Why is that your decision to make?" Madrigal narrows her eyes. "You are not Mother. You are not anyone's mother. And if there is a guardian to the queen, it is clearly meant to be my Jules." She says nothing else. She turns and walks with light steps onward up the road.

Neither Caragh nor Matthew move until Madrigal is gone. Caragh clenches her fists. She would like to jump up and down and scream.

"She thinks she can come here and upend everything! She arrives, ruins things, and leaves. That is what she does. And she never sees the consequences!"

Matthew slips his arm about her trembling waist.

"You're still her aunt," he says. "Jules still loves you. She always will."

A heaviness forms in her throat as he speaks. She knows that. She knows she is being ungrateful, spurning the idea of being only Juillenne's aunt after raising her for six years. To want Jules to run to her, not Madrigal, when she calls her first great fish or has a bad dream.

"Go home, Matthew," Caragh says.

"What? Why?"

"Because that's the first stupid thing you've ever said to me."

For days and nights, the old tales of the queens haunt Jules's every moment. She has heard the tales before—brutal, exciting stories of poison and wolves and fire. But they were only stories. Even when Arsinoe came to them and Arsinoe was real, her young mind could not fathom that one day Arsinoe would be a part of one of those stories. Joseph tries to distract her, but not even he can keep her from worrying.

"Your mum was probably fooling about. To scare us. Like around the Reaping Moon fires," Joseph says. "And even if she wasn't, Arsinoe's tough." He shoves Arsinoe, standing beside him, until she stumbles, to illustrate the point. "I wouldn't want to fight her."

But it is not just a fight. Arsinoe and Joseph would rather not know. They would rather forget the silliness that Madrigal said and go back to enjoying their summer. To believe it meant difficulty. It meant things that they were not prepared for.

It meant growing up.

Later that night, when Jules kneels down on the rug beside her grandpa Ellis's chair, she is not sure what she wants to hear. She only knows she must find out where the truth lies, in all the tales.

"Grandpa," she says, twisting a bit of the fine yarn he spins around her index finger. "What's going to happen to Arsinoe?"

He looks down at her through the bottom of his spectacles. Unlike other adults, he does not tell her that it is nothing. He does not lie.

"You have heard something," he says, "haven't you?"

"Only thinking about the old stories. The queen stories. And Arsinoe is a queen. Is she a queen like that?"

"You are still young, Jules, and this will be hard for you to understand. But as the Ascension draws nearer, you will hear things. About the contest between the queens. About how they take their crown. The people will start to talk more as Arsinoe grows."

His tone is calm. The Ascension is nothing new. The deaths of queens are nothing new. Jules feels deeply ashamed suddenly, of her youth and her ignorance. Her inability to understand what was true until now. Even knowing, it seems impossible when all the death she has ever known was the death of animals or of the old. Of fishers lost at sea or folk taken by illness or accident. But death cannot touch Arsinoe, who is young and careful. Who has become her best friend and foster sister.

"She has to?" Jules asks. "Can't someone else?"

No. It can only be her. Arsinoe is a queen, Jules. She is special. It is in her nature; you will see. It is her purpose."

That night, lying in bed with Arsinoe snoring across the room, Jules cannot stop thinking about Grandpa Ellis's words. Kill or be killed. That is her purpose. Her nature. But that is not fair. That cannot be.

"I will find a way to keep you safe, Arsinoe. I'll protect you. I promise."

THE AFTERMATH OF
ARSINOE'S ATTEMPT
TO ESCAPE

Two Years Later

INDRID DOWN

--- ⚜ ---

*T*he foolish little naturalist queen tried to flee. She, a Milone brat, and a Wolf Spring boy were found stranded in the mists, floating in a pitifully small, stolen boat. After they were caught, they were brought under lock and key to the Volroy, along with Cait Milone and her family.

"They have arrived only just now?" Natalia asks as she and Genevieve walk quickly through the castle to the chamber where the trial is to be held. "A shame. They should have been allowed to languish a while in the cells."

"The council was too eager to punish them," says Genevieve.

"Then they may be disappointed. We cannot punish the queen. Queens are not to be touched until after the Quickening, and she is still only eleven years old. The island will view it as nothing more than youthful indiscretion." Some will even admire her rebelliousness. The alliances of the island have begun to shift. Natalia has felt it ever since the elemental queen showed so strong a gift. The poisoners, her family, had ruled Fennbirn well. But they had been in power too long. Three poisoner queens, and it is easy for the island to turn restless.

Natalia and Genevieve climb the stairs and burst through the upper chamber door. The room is vast and open to the east with a railed balcony that overlooks the courtyard and on past the rooftops to Bardon Harbor. Members of her Black Council, which is finally truly hers now and not her mother's, stand in small groups in their silk handkerchiefs and deep purple skirts. Where once they were all old poisoners—except for her cousin Lucian, and Paola Vend, from the strongest poisoner family in Prynn—now the council is filled with youth: Natalia's brother Antonin and sister, Genevieve. Her younger cousin Allegra. The vivacious young poisoner Lucian Marlowe.

In the center of the room, pressed to their knees on the red, circular rug, are the naturalist queen and her co-conspirators. They are still children to her eye, though the queen and Juillenne Milone both glare at her with foolishly little fear. Natalia could have the little Milone poisoned. And the boy as well. They have committed a dire offense, and she would so very much like to give them to Katharine as a set to practice on.

As she thinks this, she glances at Juillenne Milone and nearly startles. The girl's gaze is so intense that she must be able to read Natalia's thoughts.

"We would speak," says Cait Milone. It has been a long time since Natalia has seen her, but she seems as hard and proud as ever.

"Then speak," Natalia says "Though I do not know what you think you can say."

Still, she listens as Cait pleads, insofar as Cait is capable of pleading, and turns a sympathetic ear to the tears of the boy's mother, a woman named Annie Sandrin. Mostly though, she watches. She watches the way the two younger Milone women cling to the backs of chairs but not to each other. She sees the guilt-bent back of Cait's husband. The confused, pale faces of the Sandrin men as they wonder how their boy got mixed up in a queen's business.

And she watches the queen. Arsinoe. She has grown long and lanky in the five years since the Black Cottage. Her hair is chopped short, the ends uneven, and she is not a beauty, like her queen Katharine, or like the elemental Queen Mirabella is rumored to be. She is plain, with a stingy, downturned mouth, and the council's spies in Wolf Spring say her gift has still to show.

To Natalia she looks like an easy kill.

"Natalia?" Genevieve prods her from her reverie. Apparently, the pleading and lamentation is over.

"Will the queen be allowed to speak?" asks Cait.

"It is not necessary to let the children speak," says Cousin Lucian.

"But I *would* speak."

Heads turn as Arsinoe gets to her feet.

"Then of course, Queen Arsinoe," Natalia says. "We will hear you."

"None of this was their fault." Arsinoe gestures to the

Milone girl and the dark-haired boy. "It was my idea. I told them to do it. I made them help me."

Natalia does not believe her for a moment. But she will pretend. It would be perhaps too much to ask of Katharine yet anyway, to poison two children so close to her own age.

"If that is true, then they will not die." Natalia looks at the two of them, the boy afraid and contrite, and the Milone girl still defiantly scowling. Everything about her screams defiance, except the desperate way she clings to the boy's hand. "Joseph Sandrin will be banished to the mainland until he comes of age, or we see fit to retrieve him."

Queen Arsinoe's mouth falls open, but Juillenne Milone begins to shout, and every Milone in the room presses forward, as if to comfort her.

"She has quite the temper, Cait," Natalia says. "You look almost frightened!" She raises her chin to Juillenne. "The Milone girl is sentenced to the Black Cottage. She will repay this crime through service as the next Midwife to the crown."

"No!" Arsinoe and the boy start to cry and throw their arms around Juillenne. One of the younger Milone women slumps into her seat. Another bursts through the barrier of guards, and before Natalia can stop her, attaches herself to her sleeve.

"Please," she says. "Let me go instead."

"You should be glad. She could be dead. And there are many priestesses who would be thrilled by such a sentence. It is more honor than she deserves."

"She is only a child. Have you no mercy? Are the Arrons truly as wicked as that?"

Natalia looks at her council of poisoners. The ill will toward them spreads by the day. So much so that she may have to dismiss some of them and appoint new members of other gifts. A warrior, perhaps. Or even someone giftless. That ought to appease the people.

"Very well," she says, and sighs. "That will do."

Katharine runs to greet Natalia the moment she comes through the front door, as she often does when she is not ill from poison training. Natalia stifles a smile and takes her time getting out of her gloves before lifting the cool glass of poison juice from Edmund's silver tray. Katharine seems about to burst standing there, hands folded and trembling over her black skirt and ankles twisting in an odd little dance.

"Yes, Kat?" Natalia says finally, and Katharine takes her by the hand.

"They tell me something has happened! Something with Queen Arsinoe!"

Genevieve catches Natalia's eye as she slips past in the foyer. "I will speak to the servants again about gossiping."

Natalia nods. Katharine's memories have faded. There is little danger in speaking of Arsinoe, or even Mirabella. They are only names to her now. Rivals. Though they have only discussed it in the broadest terms, Katharine knows that the other queens must be killed, and after five more years of training, and armed with a strong poisoner gift, she will be ready to do it.

"It was not the servants' fault," Katharine says quickly. "I was eavesdropping."

"Eavesdropping," Genevieve scoffs. "It is more likely that you were just silent for so long they forgot you were there, little mouse. I will speak to them." She touches Natalia's arm and leaves. Natalia gave her younger sister a place on the council only recently, but it seems to have centered her. Or at least she does not seem half as frivolous as she did before.

"What did Queen Arsinoe do?" Katharine asks. "They said that she was to be punished. That you were to punish her."

"She tried to leave the island."

"But queens are not allowed to leave the island."

"I do not even think that it was her fault." Natalia sighs. "Certainly it was not her idea. She was taken in by foolish naturalists. They have never been fit guardians."

"Not like you." Katharine looks down. She is so meek. So sweet. They ought to train that meekness out of her, but Natalia cannot bring herself to try. Or perhaps she knows that it would be impossible. Katharine will always be a kind, grateful girl in need of looking after. "So you were merciful, then? If it was not her fault?"

"I was."

"But you did punish her?"

"I did." Natalia reaches out and touches the queen's pale cheek. "I will always take care of everything, Kat. If you are tired, I will be alert. If you are weak, I will become twice as strong. I will guard your crown for you."

ROLANTH

"Queen Mirabella, I have brought you something." Luca takes down the hood of her light traveling cloak, and the queen sets aside her book and walks quickly into the High Priestess's open arms. She squeezes the girl tightly and steps back to remove her gloves. Fall has come early to Rolanth, so far in the north, with a chill wind rushing through the evergreens and across the basalt cliffs. In the capital of Indrid Down, from whence she came, they are still enjoying the last of a balmy summer, and the change in climate has made the bones in the High Priestess's wrists ache. This Rolanth weather will take some getting used to.

"I care only that you have brought yourself," Mirabella says, and kisses her hands. "But what did you bring me?"

"Iced anise cookies." Luca holds them up, in a pretty striped box, and Mirabella takes them. She sniffs the edge. "I thought we could have them with our tea. But first, to business. I must tell you what has happened to your sister, Queen Arsinoe."

Mirabella's smile fades. They have come a long way from water spirits forced down Luca's throat. Mirabella is no longer a danger. No longer kept in a basement out of fear. But the queen is stubborn. At least as stubborn as she is strong, and that makes her the most stubborn girl on the island.

"They should have known she would get herself into trouble. They should have guarded her more closely. Do they not know her at all?"

"They know her, and they care for her," Luca says. "I have seen it."

Luca takes her arm and walks with her through the open air of Rolanth Temple. As the years passed, she has grown fond of the elemental queen. More than fond. She has grown to love her, and the favoritism shown by the High Priestess cannot be denied. But favoritism by the High Priestess is not the same as favoritism by the temple. So she told Natalia Arron when the woman finally confronted her. She will never forget the look on Natalia's face when she said she would be leaving Indrid Down to reside in Rolanth with the queen.

"What was the punishment?" Mirabella asks as they walk past the altar and into the dome with the mural of elemental Queen Elo, the fire breather, where they might hide from the wind. "Was it as bad as you feared?"

"It was not. It was a rare show of Arron mercy. Banishment to the mainland for the boy." She pauses as Mirabella puts a hand to her throat. "And banishment of another kind for the girl. To the Black Cottage, to serve as the next Midwife. However, it seems that the girl's aunt will take her place, so Queen Arsinoe may keep her companion."

Mirabella exhales. After their first meeting on the banks of Starfall Lake, Luca did not know if she could be controlled. But the key to taming Mirabella has been to use a soft hand. Not to try to drive the thoughts of her sisters from her head, but to understand them. To educate her in the ways of a queen and devote her to the Goddess completely. To make her a servant.

Sara Westwood still foolishly hopes that one day Mirabella will forget, like other queens do. But Mirabella will never forget. Perhaps it is because she is such a rare queen, of such tremendous power, and the memories are the way the Goddess has chosen to test her. Or perhaps it is because her sisters were burned into her mind after being locked in a dark basement for three long years.

It will take time, and more education, but Mirabella will be the queen that the island needs. She is chosen. Luca knows that as surely as she has known anything since the day she took the bracelets and entered the temple.

"You are still wild." Luca reaches out and flicks a long lock of tangled black hair from the queen's shoulder. "Have you been out in the wind, running along Shannon's Blackway again, with Bree?"

"Only before prayer this morning. We were both so restless, awaiting your return."

"Come, then. I am restless as well after days in the carriage.

Will you walk with an old woman, down toward the city? On the evergreen path?"

"Of course, High Priestess." Mirabella offers her arm.

Luca does not really need the arm. Not yet. Her old legs are still sturdy and show no sign that they will fail her for years to come. But it is good for the queen to feel necessary. Like a caretaker. They wander down the evergreen path, in the hills that overlook the city of Rolanth. Not too far, Luca hopes, for the way back will not be quite so easy, but luckily, they come across the funeral procession just after the third curve.

"What's this now?" Luca asks, and holds up her arm.

The carriages draped in crimson slow and stop, the horses bracing against the slope of the hill as their drivers set the brake. Three carriages, of average quality, the crimson hanging in dyed wool and not something finer like silk or even muslin. They are local folk, Rolanth people. Shopkeepers or weavers. Luca does not know for sure. She only knows that one of their own committed a crime and was poisoned to death for it.

A woman steps down from the first carriage and immediately kneels before Luca. She is cloaked all in crimson and her cheeks are tear-streaked.

"High Priestess, will you bless us?"

"Of course, of course," says Luca as Mirabella looks on. "But what has happened?"

"My oldest boy, put to death for theft," the woman says. "The Black Council is cruel. Unfeeling. They tortured him with their vile concoctions!" The woman begins to wail, and

Mirabella touches her shoulder.

"Theft?" the queen asks. "But that is monstrous! To put someone to death for theft!"

Monstrous indeed. Also untrue. Luca knows the boy was tried for murder, just as she knew his funeral procession was to pass by this way, for blessings upon his body at the temple before being burned atop the Blackway Cliffs. She walks to the second carriage, the hearse carriage where the boy's body is held, and says, "Stay back, Mirabella," knowing full well that she will follow.

Luca opens the door. The corpse is covered in crimson cloth and perfumed against the scent of rot. But the scent is still there, after so many days traveling from Indrid Down. She raises her chin and pulls back the sheet.

Behind her, Mirabella gasps.

He is nothing but blisters. Broken, red blisters and deep, angry claw marks from his own fingers as he tried to dig the poison out of himself. Luca lets the queen look just a few moments longer, but covers the boy before Mirabella begins to weep. She is still young, after all. Not even twelve years old.

Luca makes sure that her face is strained as she goes back to the grieving mother, who must truly be his mother, or at least a very talented actress. She places her hands on the woman's shoulders and draws her to her feet.

"Blessings upon your boy as he rejoins the fold of the Goddess." Luca presses her thumb to the woman's forehead. "Blessings upon you. Blessings upon your family."

"It is not fair," the woman cries. "The Black Council! The poisoners!"

"I know. It is horrible. But it will not remain so. The next queen will change it."

"She must," says the woman. "This cannot stand. We cannot take it."

Luca turns sadly to Mirabella, whose eyes are wide and shining. The queen holds her head high, angry as well as horrified, just as Luca wants.

"I will change it," Mirabella says. "I promise I will change it."

Epilogue:
WOLF SPRING

Two Years Later

*A*rsinoe and Jules walk through the meadow beside
Dogwood Pond. There is no one watching them.
They have no escort. They have not even told anyone where
they are going or when they will be home. Arsinoe thought that
after what happened, after Jules and Joseph stole that boat and
tried to flee the island with her, they would be guarded night
and day. Instead, it is the opposite, as if they are barely seen.

Since Caragh departed for the Black Cottage, and Joseph
sailed away to his banishment, so much sadness emanates
through the Milone house, and all of Wolf Spring, that it is like
the peoples' hearts have slowed their beating.

"What do you want to do?" Arsinoe asks. "Go fishing?
Swimming? The water's still warm enough. Look for berries
left in Pace's ditch?"

"Sure," Jules says. But she does not say which. And there is no fire in her voice, though she does turn to Arsinoe and smile. Good Jules. She has done everything she can to let Arsinoe know that she does not blame her. But Jules's blame does not matter. Arsinoe knows that what happened to Caragh and Joseph was her fault. They were punished because they tried to save her.

Late at night, when she lies in her bed in the room she shares with Jules, Arsinoe still thinks about that day in the capital. That look on Natalia Arron's face when she banished Joseph and Caragh. How Arsinoe hates the Arrons, every one of them, with their cold, blond coloring and imperious eyes. She would like to ruin everything for them, like they have ruined everything for Jules and the Milones. She does not know how she will do it yet, but she has time. The queens' Ascension does not begin for another three years.

"I'm tired of the same old paths," Jules says suddenly, and stops short. "Let's go into the woods. Northeast, into the woods."

"All right."

Arsinoe does not like the northeastern woods. They are dark and too heavily shaded. Large creatures dwell there, safe from the noises and people in town, and whenever they go there, they hear many, lumbering or crashing through the brush, just out of sight. Of course she does not say so to Jules. They would be the most unnaturalist words ever uttered by a naturalist.

Jules leads her deeper and deeper into the forest, walking so fast that she may have forgotten that Arsinoe is with her at all. In the thick trees, Arsinoe loses track of the sun in the sky, and all the light seems slanting. Now and then, Jules stops to sniff the air and listen, but all Arsinoe hears are the whisper of leaves and the low, irritating buzz of insects. Where are the birds? Why is Madrigal's familiar, Aria, not flapping somewhere overhead, cawing in the branches?

"Look." Jules points.

Without Arsinoe noticing, they have come upon a clearing. The sun beams down upon an oblong stretch of green grass and moss, and shrub bushes with shiny, waxen leaves. In the center of it is a large, flat stone, just tall enough to climb on.

"I've never seen that before," Arsinoe remarks.

Jules does not reply. Her face is set in concentration, her blue and green eyes intent on the stone. She wipes a bit of sweat from her upper lip. Bits of her wavy brown hair have come loose from her braid, and she looks as wild as anything in the woods.

Jules walks toward the stone. Arsinoe follows and watches as she scrambles up it to stand. Jules looks around, but it does not really make her that much taller, and certainly not tall enough to see over the trees.

"This is a strange rock." Arsinoe lays her hands on it, flat and sun-warm. "So squared off and flat. Do you think it used to be something? Part of something old?"

Jules looks down at the stone.

"I think . . . if after today, we were to come looking, we would never find it again."

Arsinoe swallows as a chill passes from her scalp to her tailbone. To hide it, she climbs up onto the rock beside Jules.

"Let's just . . . stay here awhile," Jules says, and sits. "I don't feel like going home."

With the heat of the stone against their backs, and the soft sunlight on their faces, it does not take long for Jules and Arsinoe to fall asleep. When Jules wakes, it is from a good dream that she cannot quite remember, but there was laughter in it, and warmth. She thinks that Joseph and Caragh might have been there.

In the brush to her left, back in the shady cover of the trees, something rustles, and Jules sits up. She holds an arm out over the queen, ready to protect her or tell her to run. Jules is not much to look at, with her short legs and funny eyes, but she is brave. She will not hesitate to fight for Arsinoe. She is not afraid to be hurt.

But after a moment, her apprehension fades. It changes to a sensation of deep calm. Peace. The brush and ferns rustle again, and Jules waits, holding her breath.

The fuzzy mountain cat cub creeps cautiously into the light. It blinks its eyes, so young that they are still a little blue, and stands on big, fluffy paws. Its coat is the spotted coat of a baby.

Anyone but Jules would still be afraid, for where a mountain cat cub goes, a mountain cat mother is not far behind. But as Jules and the cub stare at each other, something clicks into place.

"Camden," Jules says, and the little cub bounds joyfully across the meadow and leaps into her arms.

THE

ORACLE

QUEEN

No Sight no sound

No fault was found

No treason to be had

—

Yet every one

Would die that day

For Elsabet, the mad

—From "The Song of the Mad Oracle"

PROLOGUE

On a warm summer day, Queen Mirabella sat on the front steps of the Black Cottage at Midwife Willa's feet, having her hair braided. Her little sisters—Queen Arsinoe, younger by mere minutes, and Queen Katharine, younger by a full half hour—played together in the yard.

"It is a good thing that black does not show grass marks," Willa commented when Katharine tripped over her own feet and tumbled, dark skirt flying.

"Ha ha," Arsinoe taunted. Katharine's large eyes began to shine and wobble. Mirabella cleared her throat, and Arsinoe glanced at her guiltily. Then Arsinoe sighed and went to help their youngest sister up.

"Why do you not ever tell them to be nice?" Mirabella asked.

"I tell them to be polite." Willa separated the little queen's hair with gentle fingers. "It is so long now. So long and so shiny.

When you are queen, you must wear it down often and never cover it with a veil."

Mirabella fought the urge to jerk her head. Even at five years old, she knew that nice and polite were not the same things, though she could not explain exactly why.

Down in the grass, Arsinoe and Katharine had resumed chasing each other. They laughed breathlessly, and when they ran out of laughter, Katharine began to sing a song that Willa had taught them that morning.

"No Sight, no sound, no fault was found, no treason to be had!"

"Yet every one would die that day for Elsabet the mad!" Arsinoe finished the rhyme and raised a stick she had been carrying as a sword. Katharine squealed and ran.

"Why did you teach us that song?" Mirabella asked. It was a queen's song, the tale of the last oracle queen, but Mirabella did not like it.

"Everyone on the island knows the story of the mad oracle. A queen certainly should."

"It is only a song."

"Songs preserve history. So people remember." Willa lowered her voice, and Mirabella knew that what would follow was only for her ears. "They say that Queen Elsabet's gift of sight turned on her. That it drove her mad, until in a fit of paranoia she ordered the execution of three whole houses of people."

"What is 'paranoia'?"

"Being afraid of or convinced of something that is not there."

"Were they sure she was wrong?"

"They were sure. And for her crime, Queen Elsabet spent the last twenty years of her reign locked in the West Tower of the Volroy. And now we will have no more sight-gifted queens."

Mirabella swallowed. She knew why that was. Because every triplet born with the sight gift was drowned. "All because of her?"

Willa peered around and chuckled at the stark look on Mirabella's face. "Do not be so troubled! It was a long time ago."

"How long ago?"

"Long, long ago. Before even the mist came to protect us. Queen Elsabet ruled when Fennbirn was part of the world still. Back then, the ports were crowded with ships from countries like noble Centra, rich Valostra, and warlike Salkades."

Centra, Valostra, Salkades. Names Mirabella had heard before in Willa's teachings. But not often. Those names had been lost to the mist. They were all the mainland now. They barely existed.

"Twenty years is a long time to be locked away," Mirabella murmured, and Willa kissed the top of her head. She felt a tug on the ends of her hair, and a finished braid appeared, tossed over her shoulder.

"Never mind that. Go on now and play."

Mirabella stood and did as she was told. But for the rest of that day, and many days afterward, she thought about Queen Elsabet and the song of the mad oracle. And she wondered how much of it was true.

THE QUEEN'S COURT

❦

500 Years Ago

*B*y midmorning, the Queen's Court was already a flurry of activity. Foreign ambassadors and representatives from the best families in the capital had begun to gather since the moment the doors had been thrown open. They gathered and chatted, in their best mantles and hats, exchanging news and gossip as they waited for the queen. But the queen was nowhere to be found.

"How long do you think it will be today?" Sonia Beaulin asked as she sat at the long table with the rest of the Black Council, flipping a dagger in one hand and then using her war gift to drive it into the wood.

"Not nearly as long as it will take someone to craft a new table." The elemental, Catherine Howe, raised her eyebrow at the gouges. "Be patient. You have seen how she governs; she is decisive. She doesn't need the time that other queens do. And she is still young. Still settling."

"She's had three years. And we are a young Black Council. Have we not settled?"

"You were settled to begin with," Catherine said, and tossed her pretty brown curls.

Beside them, seated at the center of the table between war-gifted Sonia and sight-gifted Gilbert Lermont—the queen's own foster brother—the poisoner Francesca Arron listened. Arrons were, as a rule, very good at listening. And waiting. And Francesca had waited for three years, since her appointment to the Black Council, to be named as its head.

"The queen arrives! Make way!"

Francesca stood with the others as Queen Elsabet and her party entered the room, their flushed cheeks and boisterous voices brightening it at once, even though the open, pillared walls of the summer court were already bathed in sunlight.

"My apologies for keeping you waiting," Queen Elsabet announced. She was dressed in hunting clothes, her black skirt loose for riding and edged in dirt. She tugged her hands free of her riding gloves and passed them to her maid with a whisper, and the girl ran, no doubt to return with sweets and savories and good wine. Clever queen, to ply them with treats. Soon her lateness would be forgotten.

She walked through the crowd quickly, her legs long enough that most of her party had to jog to keep pace. All of them except her Commander of Queensguard, of course. War-gifted

Rosamund Antere, of the Antere family of warriors, stood a head above even the queen.

"You have been hunting," Francesca said as Queen Elsabet sat down.

"I have." Her face still glowed from exertion, and her black eyes glittered. It was almost enough to make her appear beautiful. But not quite.

Sonia Beaulin cleared her throat. "Your attendants said you rode out before dawn."

"Do you know a better time to hunt for grouse?" Elsabet smiled. "Now, if my council is finished interrogating me about my sport . . ." She turned away toward her subjects, and one by one the Black Council sank to their seats, Francesca the last.

Gilbert Lermont stood and read from his ledger the names of those who had arrived first, and they stepped forward. The queen listened with rapt attention as they gave her their news: reporting achievements of trade or crops or the birth of a new high-ranking daughter. It was true what Catherine Howe said: the queen was decisive of manner. Her comments were few but earnest. She was clever but spared little time for flattery, of herself or for those she spoke to.

It was a fine enough way to rule, Francesca noted, but it would not endear her to the people at large. And for someone so decisive, she was taking plenty of time to appoint Francesca to her deserved head of council seat.

She watched the queen laugh her throaty laugh, a deep laugh for a queen so young, still a girl, really, at barely twenty.

Some said she was handsome, but they were only being kind. Queen Elsabet had an angled nose and a large mouth; she was no beauty. Not that beauty was required in queens, but a beautiful queen was easier to love.

When Elsabet's laugh turned into a cough and she excused herself from court, Francesca masked a smile. She could wait for her head of council seat. But she would not wait forever.

THE QUEEN'S GARDEN

———————— ❦ ————————

*L*ater that day, Queen Elsabet, the Oracle Queen, sat in her green rectangular garden on the southwest side of the Volroy castle. She was reclined in a soft chair at a gray stone table, playing cards with her closest companions, shaded from the sun by a black cloth canopy.

"Gilbert, are you going to discard? Or wait until I simply forget what game it is we are playing?"

Gilbert's thin lips drew together, thinning them still further, as he considered his hand. He lay a card, and she grinned and snatched it up.

"Just what I needed."

"Blast." He frowned and tousled his dark gold hair. "I'm out of practice. Few of these fools will take a card game with someone sight-gifted. As if that is how it works."

"Indeed. One does not need the sight to beat play as bad as yours." With a light laugh, Elsabet set her winning hand before him on the table.

"Blast."

She smiled as he gathered up the cards and began to shuffle. Gilbert Lermont was her foster brother; they had grown up together in the white city of Sunpool, and she could count on one hand the number of times he had beaten her at cards. But let him blame it on lack of practice. She knew how he felt, alone in a new city with few other oracles.

"I have been thinking often of home," she said.

Gilbert glanced at her from beneath his dark eyebrows. So did Bess, her favorite maid and constant companion, and Rosamund Antere, always nearby as her Commander of Queensguard.

"Indrid Down is home now, Elsie."

Elsabet frowned. "Can one not have two homes? I just . . . I miss being there, before all of this." She gestured to her head, to the silver crown set with cloudy stones that felt melted to her head. "I miss being near those who know what the sight gift is and how it works. People here look at me like an oddity. And they expect every day at court to be a wonder. As if I ought to be spouting grand prophecy twice in the afternoon and once before breakfast."

She took up her freshly dealt cards and set them down again when Bess pushed more of Gilbert's tonic toward her in a cup.

"I do not want any more. It's bitter."

"Please," Bess said. "Your illness worries everyone."

"It was only a headache. Only dust in my chest from the hunt." But Elsabet drank the tonic down even if just to see Bess smile. "Besides, they were not worried so much as irritated."

"Perhaps if you would not arrive late so often," Gilbert said as he arranged his hand.

"That wouldn't change a thing. My Black Council does not like me because I do not do things the way they want me to. But weren't you the one who told me, Gilbert, that I should make my mark as queen the instant I arrived at the Volroy? The moment I took my crown. Weren't you the one who warned me that young queens are not taken seriously? That it could take years before I was truly the ruler of my island?"

"Was it not also me who warned you that a queen is only as good as her advisers?"

"Yes." She crooked her mouth at him. "But you were wrong. That may be true of other queens, but an oracle queen is only as good as her gift."

At the corner of the canopy, ever watchful, Rosamund Antere cocked her head of bloodred hair.

"Rosamund? What is it?"

"Your king-consort approaches."

Elsabet's heart thrummed in her chest, and she cursed it silently. She was a queen, not some village girl who could let her heart dictate her behavior. But with William, her king-consort, that was a difficult thing to remember. Every time he walked into a room she held her breath. Every time he looked at her, she wanted to hide her unattractive face behind her hand.

William was from Centra, a country across the seas to the northeast. It boasted a fine army and bountiful croplands. A king-consort from Centra was always a politically savvy selection. Though to tell the truth, Elsabet would have chosen William even if he had come from nothing.

Other suitors had been handsome. All of them, actually. And several had been dashing. But none of them looked at Elsabet the way William had. No one in her whole life had looked at her like that. Like she was beautiful. Desirable. And certainly no one as attractive as he was, with his bright blue eyes and midnight hair. When they were courting, he used to say that on the throne their black hair would make them as finely matched as a set of carriage horses.

He entered the canopy and one of Elsabet's attendants quickly brought him a seat. Though it was probably a waste of time. William never stayed in one place for long. He was a man of sport. It had been at his insistence that they rose before dawn to hunt for grouse that morning.

He bent and kissed the queen's cheek, but when she frowned, he turned her face and kissed her lips instead. "These are for you." He set a bundle of wildflowers on the tabletop, pretty blooms of pink and white and yellow, their stems cut evenly by his dagger and tied with a length of striped ribbon.

"I picked them from the riverbank near where I was swimming," he said as Elsabet sniffed, and indeed, the cloth around his collar was still wet.

Elsabet fingered the ribbon. It was an expensive adornment, a new fashion that she had seen many of the daughters from well-gifted families wearing.

"Where did you get the ribbon?" she asked, and William

swallowed. "Did you go by the market?"

"Yes! I couldn't very well present you with a loose bundle."

Elsabet tried to smile. She gestured to the cards. "Shall we deal you in?"

"No." William chewed his lip. "I crave some music. I think I'll go and secure us a few musicians." Then he was gone, with no more than a glance, and Elsabet half rose out of her chair to follow him. But he did not disappear completely. He lingered in the garden, chatting with a few of the people who had gathered near the queen's party in small conversational parties of their own. Elsabet's throat tightened as he touched the chin of a very pretty elemental girl with a bright blond bun.

"You know he has always been flirtatious," Gilbert said quietly. "That was one of the qualities that drew you to him when he was only a suitor."

Elsabet tore her eyes away from William and forced herself to play a card. "Gilbert, does your sight gift now extend to mind reading?"

"No, my queen."

"I didn't think so." Gilbert's gift was for visions in smoke, along with the uncanny ability to find things he sought, that manifested in a near-trance state and caused him to sway strangely back and forth. His sight gift did not extend to hearing the thoughts of others or sensing their emotions. Her gift did not extend to that either, and she was glad of it.

Forcing herself to ignore William, Elsabet leaned back to look up at the grandness of the castle. Or rather, the grandness that was to come. The great fortress of the Volroy had been under construction for a hundred years, and still the heights of the towers were not complete. For a hundred years, black stone had made its way across the island, over land and down river and around the sea to Bardon Harbor. A hundred years and countless changes of master builders and craftsmen and laborers. But under Elsabet, it would be finished. She knew it, because she had seen it. In the same vision that showed her she would best her sisters and become the Queen Crowned. She saw herself in a vision wandering the rooms of the completed West Tower, with a crown upon her head.

"There will be black spires atop them soon," she said, and Bess followed her gaze upward. "Did you know, Bess, that it was the war queen, Aethiel, who began construction of the Volroy?"

"I know it," Gilbert answered before Bess could reply. "Aethiel began it, and elemental Elo, the fire breather, continued it, and so did our last queen, the warrior Emmeline."

"Of course you know that." Elsabet shoved him playfully to knock the smugness out of his expression. "You are a historian. But make sure the commonfolk know it, too, will you? I think they are beginning to resent the expense."

"Your reign is bound to be less expensive than those of the war queens," Gilbert said, "with their constant raids and battles."

At the mention of war, Rosamund spoke quickly, surprising them all that she had been bothering to listen. "The people understand war. They understand its costs. Its glory." She shrugged. "And the spoils don't hurt either."

"Would you have me be a war queen, then, Rosamund?"

Rosamund turned her head and regarded the queen with steady green eyes. She smiled. "I would not have you be anything but what you are."

"Good." Elsabet smiled back, her gaze flitting past William, who was returning with his found musicians. "Because the time of the war queens is over. Now we shall have peace. The island has earned it."

THE BLACK GREEN

❧

*I*n the summer months, it was not uncommon for the queen to hold court or entertain guests outdoors. She favored the garden known as the Black Green, a rectangular space bordered by hedges and a stone wall on the north, with soft, cropped green grass and few trees. Wide, gravel paths cut through from every corner and converged at a dark stone fountain. Inevitably, one of the foreigners would quip that the Black Green was not very black, and the queen would reply that they could not very well call it "the Green Green." Everyone would laugh, and Francesca Arron would ball her hands into fists. Most people, even most of the Black Council, found the outdoor courts rather pleasant. But to Francesca Arron, it was yet another way that Elsabet bucked tradition.

Francesca stood apart from the others, watching as the queen entertained the ambassador from Valostra and his four companions. The queen having chosen a king-consort from the

135

rival nation of Centra, there was not much for the Valostrans to do there. The bulk of Fennbirn's trade and resources were reserved for the country of the king-consort. But the Valostrans had no shortage of coin and continued to send representatives regardless, in the hopes of maintaining good relations until the next Ascension began.

"Well done, Queen Elsabet!" The ambassador clapped when the queen's ball struck the painted pole they had stuck into the ground. It was a game played with the feet, and to do it well, Elsabet had drawn her skirts up nearly to the knee.

"Careful," Sonia Beaulin said as she approached to offer Francesca a bundle of poison berries. She held up a small dish of honey to dip them in. "Your scowl is beginning to show through your artfully constructed expression."

"Humph." Francesca stuffed a sweetened berry into her mouth. "Look at her. Just look at her. Playing their games with her dress hiked up to her head."

"It's nowhere near her head. And her legs are not bare. Nothing that could be considered inappropriate."

"Not inappropriate here. But in their country? They will return to Valostra and say the queen is indecent. A harlot."

"Then let them return," Sonia said, her war gift bristling, "with their tongues cut out."

"Once again, you miss the point. I care not for their opinion and have no respect for their ridiculous standards of conduct. But reports like that are what bring the soldiers to our shores. War, to root out our indecency and corruption. To save our souls." Francesca spat a berry seed upon the ground. "There is nothing I hate more than an attack and slaughter meant to save us from ourselves."

At the mention of battle, Sonia's eyes glittered. "Surely Queen Elsabet's sight gift would give us plenty of warning should that come to pass."

"The sight gift is unreliable. And hers is waning."

"How do you know?"

Francesca raised her eyes to Sonia's. "I just do."

A collective gasp rose as the queen, attempting to make another kick, tripped when her skirt came loose and fell to her knees. An embarrassment to be sure, but Elsabet only laughed. She brayed, really, her mouth too wide and her teeth too large. And the Valostrans were quick to help her to her feet, crowding around her in their garish striped tunics and feathered hats. It was a good thing she was a queen. Any other girl that plain they would have left in the dirt.

"Look," Francesca said. "Even the king-consort knows she is allowing too many liberties." William was smiling, but as the game went on, his smile became more and more doubtful. "He knows they will talk."

"Well, what are we to do?" asked Sonia. "We are her advisers, but she takes very little advice. Catherine says to let her settle into the crown more. Then she'll stop striving always to do things her own way. Then she'll tire of trying to make her mark."

"Catherine Howe has been smitten with the queen since

before the crowning. Just like your rival." She nodded toward the Commander of Queensguard, standing ever at the ready, monitoring her soldiers placed at each entrance.

Pleasure bloomed in Francesca's chest as Sonia bared her teeth. Such a strong hatred. Francesca liked strong emotions. Strong emotions she could use.

THE QUEEN'S CHAMBER

❧

Queen Elsabet stared into her crystal mirror. After a long day of entertaining the Valostrans, she found herself alone again, with only Bess, her favorite maid, who made the queen ready for bed. Alone, the queen's mood often became depressed, and the reflection staring back from the mirror did nothing to raise her spirits. Bess had already removed Elsabet's carefully applied makeup, and the face the queen saw was clean, unadorned.

She straightened her back and took a breath. Handsome, they called her. She was a queen of presence, they said. She hoped it was true. With such a homely face, it was all she could aspire to.

"Do you think pretty queens have an easier time of it?" Elsabet asked as Bess brushed out the queen's long, black hair. "Or must we all prance about like prized horses to impress?"

"Easier. Who wants easier? The Elsabet I know chases

challenges. She relishes them."

Elsabet sighed. So she did. When she had her first vision of the Ascension and in it saw that her youngest sister would kill their eldest sister for her, she was slightly disappointed. One less task between her and the crown. She felt like she should have done it all.

"Sweet Bess." Elsabet reached back and touched the girl's hand. She and Bess were practically the same age, but beautiful girls always seemed infinitely younger, and Bess was one of the most beautiful girls on the island, all red-gold curls and deep pink lips. "Will you stay on with me here even after you wed?"

"I am in no hurry to wed, my queen."

"Having too much fun enjoying your freedoms?"

Bess blushed. "I always thought it was one of the heaviest burdens for a queen to bear . . . that you are forced to wed so young. So soon. With so little . . . sampling."

"I didn't need to sample." Elsabet smiled. "I found William."

Someone knocked at the chamber door, and Bess set down her brush. "There he is now," she whispered into the queen's ear, and Elsabet's skin prickled. Even after three years of marriage, the arrival of her king-consort still made her shiver.

But Bess returned only with a tray.

"What's this?"

"More tonic from Gilbert." Bess set it on the bedside table and stirred a spoonful of honey into the bitter liquid. Elsabet gestured for another spoonful, and grimacing, another after that.

"Is your cough still so bad?" Bess asked as the queen sipped. "You have been taking the tonic for weeks now and even during the day."

"It is not bad. The headaches, mainly. The tonic does not do much. What could any tonic do against the stress of the crown? But you know Gilbert. He is always looking after me, always overcautious. So I will drink this bitter stuff until he is satisfied." Her eyes wandered back toward the hall. "Did you see any sign of my king-consort?"

"No, my queen."

Elsabet frowned. "Do you remember when he used to run to me every night? How he used to stand outside hopping while you dressed me for bed, complaining about the draughts in this blasted, unfinished castle?"

Bess did not reply, but Elsabet caught her reflection in the mirror. An expression of pity.

"Have you seen him with someone?"

"No, my queen," Bess said, and went quickly to add logs to the fire.

"But he has been flirting. The whole court has seen him flirting."

"The king-consort has always been flirtatious. Especially with you, Elsabet."

Especially with her. But it had been months since he had sought her out during the day so they could secret themselves off somewhere, in an unused room or an empty corridor. And if it was no longer her in the corridors with him, then it would be someone else.

"Has he made . . . advances toward you, Bess?"

Bess turned and stood up straight. The fire blazed behind her. "No. And if he did, I would strike him in the face. I would bruise him black and blue and then I would tell you at once." Elsabet did not reply right away, and Bess hurried back to the queen's side. "You do believe me?"

"Of course I do. I just wish you would have said that he would never. That my William would never do such a thing. But that would be a lie. And you will never lie to me."

Bess stroked the queen's hair gently and kissed the top of her head. "They say it is normal for a Centran man . . . and it would not be the first time that a king-consort went outside the marriage bed."

True, though normally he waited for permission first. Or at least for the queen to take a lover.

"Normal," Elsabet said. "I do not want normal. I want greatness. That's what I want my reign to be. When, Bess, have I ever been satisfied with normal?"

That night, Elsabet tossed and turned in her bed until she finally gave up and pulled on a robe. She dragged a chair across the rug and onto the stone floor beside her window and pushed it open, letting a cool breeze in to accost the fire. It was high summer, but as near as the capital was to Bardon Harbor, nights could still turn cold, and she drew her feet up to tuck her toes beneath her dressing gown.

William had never come. He was drunk somewhere or busy

with some Central matter. Perhaps caught in a late game of cards or resting for an early hunt he neglected to inform her of. Any of those excuses would be better than the truth she feared.

She rested her elbows on the sill and looked out over the sleeping city, over the calm waters of the harbor and up toward the moon. When she was a girl, it seemed to her that the Goddess was there, in the moon. In that bright, glowing light in the sky. The Goddess was everywhere, of course. In the land and in the crops, in the fish that swam upriver. In the people. And most of all, in Elsabet, her chosen queen.

"There was a time when my gift was so strong I had only to ask you for a vision and you would send one. But then there had been purpose. The Quickening. My Ascension. Do all oracle queens' gifts abandon them after they are in the crown, or is it only mine?" She waited, but the moon made no reply. It was silly, she supposed, to ask the moon for answers. But there was no one else to ask. The High Priestess was away on pilgrimage, wandering the mountains as she had for many years. And the accounts of the oracle queens who came before related only their grandest visions. Their most important prophecies. There was almost no mention of their daily governance, and certainly no passages offering advice on king-consorts who would not stay put.

"William, my William," she muttered. "I am strong in everything, except for him. One little weakness. But how it seems to overcome all else."

Elsabet waited by the window a while longer. She did not

truly know what she was waiting for. A vision from the Goddess? William to walk through her door? Her thoughts were clouded, and the moon, lovely as it was, offered no answers. So she returned to bed and, finally, slept.

And when she slept, she dreamed. A bright dream, clear and real, from the sunlight on his hair to the crunch of dirt beneath his shoes. He was a boy, a young man, in common clothes and paint-smudged fingers. He had a broad smile, a little crooked, and the dimple in his right cheek was deeper than in his left. He was not handsome like William was handsome. But his eyes were warm. He did nothing more extraordinary in the dream than smile at her, and when he spoke, it was only her name.

"Elsabet."

THE QUEEN'S COURT

he next day, Elsabet tried to pay attention to what
Gilbert was saying. It was some matter of coin,
which normally she was quite involved in, much to the rest of
the Black Council's chagrin. She gathered that the previous
queen was rather hands-off when it came to the day-to-day ruling, preferring instead to focus on the grander, broader strokes
of war raids and quests. When Elsabet came into the crown,
she thought that the Black Council would welcome her interest.
But instead they seemed to resent it. Even the young members
she appointed herself: Sonia Beaulin and Francesca Arron. Not
Catherine Howe, though. Kind, level-headed Catherine Howe
could probably not be resentful of anything.

Today, though, the council could have its way. All through
the morning session, Elsabet's answers had been clipped and
passionless. Her eyes flitted across papers presented to her
without seeing them. She was distracted, and the reason was

clear to everyone in the room.

Her king-consort had been seated at a table with a dark-haired beauty for the last hour. Except he was not quite sitting. He was leaning so far across toward her that he was less at the table than he was mounting it.

"Elsie."

Elsabet blinked. Gilbert called her that only in private. How many times had she ignored him, she wondered, to get him to resort to it before the court?

"Yes, Gilbert."

"Are you with us?"

"Of course." She motioned with her hand. "Go on." She ignored their doubtful expressions and refocused. It was not a complicated matter; she could catch up on what she had missed. Or she could if her ears were not filled with her king-consort's laughter, a sound made all the louder by the fact that he was clearly trying to muffle it.

Elsabet turned and stared at William. At her movement, the rest of the court froze. All but the king-consort and the girl whose dark curls were twirled around his fingers. The room went so silent that when Elsabet spoke, it rang through the air like a shout.

"What is so funny?"

William's and the girl's laughter cut off abruptly, and they broke apart. His hand slid back to his side of the table like a guilty snake. "Darling?" he asked, and Elsabet smiled broadly.

"What is so funny? You have been quite merry there in your

little corner. Will you not share the joke with us?"

"Ah . . ." William's mouth hung agape. "We were discussing the state of fashion. How . . . how many layers and ties and time it takes to get one properly dressed."

Properly dressed. Or quickly undressed.

"Of course." Elsabet forced a laugh. In the court, a few scared or sympathetic folk joined in. "A very funny subject indeed."

For a moment, it seemed that Elsabet would return to the matter of coin. She sat there for several long, slow breaths, her hands clenching and unclenching in her lap as she tried to master herself. But in the end, she could not. She stood and pushed away from the Black Council table, her long legs sweeping her quickly down the aisle.

"Queen Elsabet! Elsie!" Gilbert sputtered, and shuffled papers, hastening to follow her.

"That is all for today," Elsabet announced as she left. "I thank you for your attendance."

As soon as she quit the room, Bess was at her side without needing to be summoned, as was Rosamund Antere, who swung her spear in a broad circle to pave the queen's way.

"Bess, my gloves, if you please. And a carriage."

"Ready the queen's carriage!" Rosamund bellowed, and ten queensguard soldiers jumped to do her bidding.

"No," Elsabet called out. "I have changed my mind. Not the carriage. A horse. And horses for the commander and Bess."

"Elsabet." Gilbert caught up to her and took her by the

elbow. "Are you all right?"

"I'm fine, Gilbert. I am just going to take some air at the river market."

He frowned. The Black Council did not like the queen frequenting the markets like a commoner. But that is precisely why she did it: to be like her people, to be out among them. To mix with them and hear their troubles firsthand. And today, it would give her distance from William and his girl, so let the council grumble. She could never seem to please them anyway.

Sonia Beaulin appeared at the door and lifted her chin. "The river market?" She sniffed and turned her gaze on Rosamund. "You shouldn't take the queen there with such a small detail of soldiers."

"I know the layout well, Beaulin," Rosamund replied. "A small detail is plenty of protection."

"Forgive me if I do not trust the judgment of an Antere."

Rosamund stepped forward. So did Sonia, though Rosamund towered over her by a head.

"Enough, enough." Gilbert pressed them apart. "You are like dogs, you two. Snarling and snapping and your hackles always up. We ought to have appointed a naturalist to the Black Council so they could bring you to heel."

"Thank you, Gilbert," the queen said, and began to walk before anyone else could pose an objection. "I will not be gone overlong."

After the queen had left, her party following in her shadow, Sonia returned to the throne room and made her way to her friend, the poisoner Francesca Arron.

"That is the first time she has spoken against his behavior in public," she said. Then she snorted. "Look at him. How dejected his handsome face looks. He won't be able to muster the nerve to climb into a strange bed tonight."

"Perhaps tomorrow," Francesca replied. But she was not even looking at the king-consort. She was looking at the gathered people, watching them whisper. Registering the surprise on their faces at their usually composed queen's small outburst. No doubt Francesca would be devising a way to use that gossip to her advantage. Arrons were always like that. "Have the girl banished from attending court for a season," Francesca said. "And make sure you are seen doing it. The queen will appreciate that favor."

INDRID DOWN

❧

*B*y the time Elsabet reached the river market, the jolting pace of her horse had almost shaken off the feelings of jealousy and shame. The nerve of William, to flaunt his pursuit right before her eyes. And what a fool she had been, to succumb to such an embarrassing outburst. The people would whisper now, Elsabet thought as she dismounted. But let them. They had already been whispering for months. Let them see that she would not simply accept his behavior. Let them talk about that.

She took a deep breath as Bess dismounted and came to her side and Rosamund to the other. The river market was her favorite to frequent in the summer, as it was cooler, less crowded than the Bardon Harbor market, and smelled less of fish. Today it was bustling, the stalls full with merchants selling fresh and dried meats, newly dyed cloth, jewelry, and any manner of trinket the heart could desire. They smiled and doffed their hats

to the queen, and she smiled back. They had not witnessed her
shame. And she vowed that her behavior at the market would
be so carefree that none of them would believe it when they
heard the gossip later.

They stopped at a naturalist stall and watched a man ripen
strawberries by palming them with his hands. Elsabet pur-
chased a basketful. "For pies," he suggested as he took her
coins.

"A strong gift for a man, ripening those berries with a
touch," Rosamund commented as they walked. "He must be
a Travers." The Traverses were the strongest naturalist family
on the island. Most of the fruits and vegetables that made it
to the Volroy were grown and ripened by them in their city,
Sealhead, on the southwest shores of the island, for theirs were
the best.

Bess twisted her neck back to get a better look at the naturalist. She was always curious about the strongly gifted, as she
had no gift herself. To their right, a woman called out to them
with a cup of cool wine for the queen, and Rosamund nearly
knocked it out of her hand. Bess paid the woman and thanked
her, giving Rosamund a look.

"You war-gifted," she muttered. "To you everything is a
threat. Everything is a challenge."

"Would you have me be less vigilant with the safety of our
queen?"

Bess placed her hand on Elsabet's arm. "Who would think
to harm the queen? But of course not. I would simply have you

overreact less. Stop seeking a battle. We have had two queens of war out of the last three, and now there is no king anywhere who would move against us. If one did, he knows what he would find: strong-gifted warriors whose arrows never miss. And who embrace death." She touched her fingers to the bottom of Rosamund's jaw, and Rosamund swatted her away with a grin.

"We do not embrace death. We only know we're unlikely to meet it."

They wandered down the row where two men haggled over the price of pretty colored fabrics, and Elsabet ran her hand down the hanging cloth.

"I also wish you sought less of a battle, Rosamund," she said. "At least with members of my Black Council." She looked at her commander sternly so her meaning would not be lost. Too often Rosamund and Sonia Beaulin nearly came to blows. At the palace, Gilbert had said they were like dogs. But they were more like wolves. Two packs of them: the Beaulins and the Anteres, and if anything were to truly start between them, it would end in blood. When Elsabet became queen, she thought to appease both families by appointing Sonia to the Black Council and Rosamund head of the queensguard, but now it seemed that she had made a mistake and each would have preferred the other position. But then who could say? Perhaps it was their fate to be always at odds, and there could never have been any peace between them.

"I will try, Queen Elsabet."

"Good." She linked her arms in each of her friends'. "We

must all try to set examples for the people. And your reputation is fearsome enough. They still say that you dye your hair red with madder root just so it will look like blood."

"Ha!" Bess barked, and covered her mouth.

"But we do not always have to set good examples." Rosamund lowered her voice and nudged Elsabet with her shoulder. "Not with those we hold most dear. We can see that you've been troubled."

"And I thought I was so good at disguising it." Elsabet sighed. Bess and Rosamund were her closest friends. She was closer to them even than she was to Gilbert, whom she viewed as a brother. Bess had been with her since they were both young girls and Bess's mother had been in service to the Lermont family in Sunpool. Elsabet and Rosamund had been much thrown together over the course of the Ascension Year, and Elsabet had taken to the gruff soldier immediately. If she could not trust them, she could not trust anyone.

"You know they say I am unwell," she said quietly.

"The people fear you are unwell," Bess corrected, though to Elsabet there did not seem to be much of a difference. "That's why they talk. They worry."

"I think they are right."

"Right?" Rosamund turned to the queen sharply and looked up and down her body. "What's the matter? What is the ailment?"

Elsabet smiled. "Nothing you can see from the outside."

"Is this about your rake of a king-consort? Give me leave to beat him. I won't leave any marks."

"Rosamund!" Bess exclaimed, and the commander quieted. "Tell us, Elsabet."

"I think my gift is failing," Elsabet said flatly. And there it was. Her secret fear, harbored for nearly a year. A year of gradually lessening visions, and increasing coughs and headaches. "I have not had a vision or felt any touch of the sight for a very long time."

Rosamund and Bess looked at each other gravely, their steps slowing in the midst of the bustling marketplace. Elsabet shook them gently by the elbows. She should not have told them there. They will stand out in their sadness.

"How long?" Bess asked.

"Months. Many, many months." She did not mention the strange dream she had after speaking to the moon outside her chamber window. The dream of the boy with paint-smudged fingers. That was only a dream. Nothing at all. "And what is an oracle queen without a gift?"

"She is the Queen Crowned," Rosamund said. "And besides, how do you know your gift has weakened? It was strong when you needed it to Ascend. You must not have need of it now. The people should be glad that you have no visions. It means they are safe."

"But surely"—Elsabet blushed—"surely it would have warned me about William's . . . wandering."

"Why would it?" Bess blurted. "The Goddess need not send a vision for something that is so glaringly obvious." She gasped and clapped her hand over her mouth again. Elsabet's mouth hung open, but then she laughed. Loudly and genuinely, her head thrown back to show her large teeth.

"Thank you, Bess. That actually does make me feel better."

THE QUEEN'S CHAMBER

❧

When William slunk into Elsabet's chamber, she had already determined to be angry. Cold. Perhaps even aloof. It had been three days since she had caught him flirting with that girl in front of her entire court. At first, it seemed that he stayed away out of fear or perhaps courtesy. But as days went by, it began to feel more like a punishment. As if she should be the one to seek him out to beg forgiveness.

I am a queen, Elsabet thought. *I have been a queen since I was born, and there is no begging in me.*

But that was a lie. The moment she heard his footsteps at her door, she knew she would drop to her knees and plead, if only he would stop. If he would come back. If he would love her.

Bess let him into the room and squeezed Elsabet's hand before dropping a curtsy and leaving them alone.

"Well, my dearest?" William asked. "Is it time for our quarrel to end?"

The resentment in his voice broke her heart. Surely he should try to appease her. Take her hand. Not stand there straight-backed and glaring.

Elsabet breathed in slowly. "Do you want to be set aside?"

"Is that a threat?"

"Take it how you like. Do you want to be set aside? To be king-consort in name only? I am happy to furnish you a house in the country. A small estate where the hunting is good. I will make no excuses for you, but you may disappear from the capital."

He had not expected that. He looked positively bewildered. "Disappear from the capital? Into the countryside? And what will my cousin the king of Centra think of that?"

"He will think nothing of it. We will still be married. The alliance between Centra and Fennbirn is fixed, for a generation." She waited and watched him think, forcing her face to remain impassive.

"And what will you do?" he asked. "When I am gone?"

"I will do as I like. I am the queen." She was the Queen Crowned, the embodiment of the Goddess on earth. Yet that was not enough to make him look upon her as he looked upon that pretty girl in the throne room.

As she stood there silently, William started to fidget and his posture lost stiffness. "But . . . what about the triplets? The new queens?"

"You will visit my bed during every Beltane." Elsabet swallowed. "Your sacred chore."

He ran his hands roughly across his face, and at once the hardness there was gone, and he came forward and grasped her wrists. "Elsabet. Darling. Has it really come to this? Over such a small thing?"

"You shame me before my court. It is no small thing."

"I know." He kissed her face. "I know; you're right. I was thoughtless. I was carried away." He kissed her neck, her hands, her lips. He used what power he had to weaken her resolve until her arms were around him, and her gown around her waist, and he moved her to the bed.

MIDSUMMER

❧

With Midsummer approaching, the capital was a bustling, jovial place as the crown and the citizenry prepared to celebrate the festival. Elsabet intended to open the grounds of the Volroy and hold the festival feast in the courtyard instead of in Indrid Down Square. It would be open to commoners and rich, gifted families alike. A show of unity and peace after decades of war games and raids. Of course the Black Council was against it.

"The sanctity of the castle would be violated, and your own security would be impossible to assure." Sonia Beaulin scrunched her face. She did not say outright that the queen was a fool, but her exasperated expression made her feelings plain.

"Rosamund will see to my security."

"Rosamund Antere is weak-gifted at strategy. She manages the queensguard with no more competency than a child."

Beside Sonia in the Black Council chamber, elemental

Catherine Howe tugged at her sleeve. "You know she can hear you. She's right outside."

"Do you think I care!" Sonia slammed her fists onto the table, and the entire table shook.

Elsabet winced. Sweet Catherine, so mild and calm for an elemental, with so little understanding of the other gifts. She meant no harm, but she often made everything worse.

"Holding the festival in the Volroy grounds will also allow the people a closer look at the construction of the towers. I can announce that the West Tower is nearly complete. And recount the history of the build so they will remember that it was not I who ordered such an expensive castle. I have heard enough of their grumbling when I pass through the marketplaces. They think I'm bankrupting them."

"Preposterous," said Gilbert, and smoothed his wispy yellow hair away from his forehead. "The flow of materials has been steady, near constant since before we were born."

"I know that, and you know that, but the people forget."

"The people are restless," Sonia muttered. "They've been too long without war and raids. They are looking for things to grumble about."

Elsabet pursed her lips. They were getting nowhere. "I have heard your objections to the festival feast and will consider them. But Midsummer is in two weeks, and we had best begin making the castle ready." She pushed away from the council table and ignored their sour faces as she led the way to the Black Green for an afternoon of games and refreshment.

Rosamund swung the door open, her face like a storm cloud, and bowed as Elsabet passed. Her bow was good, one hand hidden in the fold of her cape, and had the queen not been searching for it, she would not have seen the hilt of Rosamund's drawn dagger.

"Walk with me, Rosamund," she said, and dragged her along. "And sheathe that knife. I won't have you slicing into Sonia Beaulin today, no matter what she said."

They reached the Black Green without incident and dispersed onto the lawn, where tables had been set with food and drink. William was already there and greeted Elsabet with a kiss on the cheek. He had been attentive since their reconciliation. He came to her bed every night the first week after, and even corralled her in the castle halls, leaning her against a tapestry and tormenting her with kisses until she could hardly think. But his ardor faded, as she knew it would. As it must. She suspected he was sneaking out with girls from the capital again. He was certainly flirting again. But at least he curbed his impulses when she was right there watching.

The queen sat with Gilbert at a table in the shade, and Bess poured them cooled wine. Elsabet drank hers and nearly spat it out. It had been laced with Gilbert's bitter tonic.

"Bleagh."

"Apologies, my queen. It was by Gilbert's order."

Elsabet patted her foster brother's hand. "And I appreciate it. But I have already taken a dose of tonic with my breakfast. So now, Bess, I would have plain, watered wine."

"Yes, Queen Elsabet." Bess curtsied. Gilbert frowned but did not argue.

"A few petitioners have come," Bess said as she poured. "I think they hoped you would be sitting for petitions in the afternoon."

"How many?"

"Only a few. None with contentious concerns. It is mostly about the festival. A baker with samples for the feast. A painter."

"Send them to me, then." Elsabet waved her hand toward the rear of the green, where she spied several figures lingering in the shadows. "The whole Black Council is here anyway."

She was only half paying attention when the boy stepped in front of her and bowed. There was nothing remarkable about him. Nothing to catch the eye. It was not until Francesca Arron read his petition that Elsabet really looked at him. And then she could not stop staring.

It was the young man from her dream. From the mussed, dark blond hair to the paint smudges on his fingers. He was real. She could still hear the exact sound of his voice from that night, when she heard him say her name.

"Queen Elsabet, this is Jonathan Denton. An apprentice painter studying beneath a master in Prynn." Francesca paused to look him over. Prynn was the poisoners' city. No doubt she was trying to ascertain whether she knew him or whether he shared any Arron blood. "State your business to the queen."

"Queen Elsabet," he said, and she nearly gasped. "I would like to paint your portrait. For the Midsummer Festival."

She made no response

"The queen does not care for having her portrait painted," Francesca said. "She was made to sit for one when she was first crowned. I see no reason to submit her to it again, certainly not so soon."

"I would—" Jonathan Denton faltered. "I work very fast."

"Thank you. But we do not need to pay for another portrait just so some young apprentice can make a name for himself."

His mouth hung open. He nodded and bowed again, looking up helplessly into the queen's wide eyes. "Thank you, my queen," he said, and turned to go.

"Wait!" Elsabet half rose from her seat. Francesca Arron looked at her sharply. "I will sit for this painter. A portrait of the first Midsummer Festival held inside the castle grounds would be a welcome addition to the Tower walls."

THE VOLROY

※

℮ lsabet truly did hate sitting for portraits. Her face had twitched nearly the entire time she sat for her first one, and she hated the finished piece, even if the artist had been kind and made her cheeks smooth and jawline delicate and softened the crook of her nose. So she did not know what she was doing when she met the painter Jonathan Denton in the bright, open courtyard that stretched before the Volroy's western side. She knew only that she had seen him in a dream, and she was determined to discover why.

"Queen Elsabet." He came as close to her as he dared and bowed. "I'm honored that you would sit for me. I promise that the portrait will be exactly as you wish. My renditions of buildings are very strong, I am told. The Volroy would make for a fine backdrop, with you seated in the foreground. Or perhaps—"

"That will be fine."

He readied a chair for her and she sat, holding patiently still as he adjusted the fall of her gown and even touched her face, moving her this way and that, to better catch the light.

"How long will this take?"

"Not long." He smiled, a little shyly. "If you are still."

"Am I free to talk?"

"Of course! I—I'll tell you when it comes time to work on your . . . expression."

She watched him as he went about his business, readying brushes and cloths and paint.

"You seem nervous."

"I am nervous."

"But you were bold enough to come to the queen and ask to paint a portrait for a special occasion."

He smiled again, easier this time. "I suppose I am bold, for my art."

Elsabet sighed. Her assessment of him remained unchanged. There was nothing extraordinary about him. He was a boy of average height and build. Her age perhaps or a few years younger. Could she have been mistaken? Was her recollection of the dream flawed? Or perhaps the dream had been only a dream. Perhaps she had seen him somewhere before, in the marketplace or in the square, and her mind had simply conjured his face from her memory, for no reason at all.

Except the dream had been so vivid. And she was not in the habit of dreaming of strangers.

"Jonathan Denton," she said. "Amuse me while you work. Tell me something of yourself."

"What would you like to know?"

"Anything. What you usually tell someone upon first meeting them. I have never heard of the Denton family," she said when he seemed to be struggling. "You apprentice in Prynn, but are you from there? Are you of the poisoner gift?"

"I am. We are, though I'm not surprised that you haven't heard of us. The Arrons are the only poisoners that anyone seems to know."

"That is because they share blood with every poisoner line, or that is what they say."

"It's true." Jonathan raised his brush. "Every poisoner in Indrid Down has a little of the Arrons in them. But I don't have much. My hair is nowhere near blond enough."

She chuckled and looked at his clothes: dark gray hose and tunic. The cloth was of good quality, and it was well-made, but it was simple and had no fur edging in sight. It was probably the finest he owned, worn especially for this occasion on the Volroy grounds. He straightened and studied her face so intently that she blushed.

"Is there," she said, and cleared her throat, "is there somewhere in particular you would have me fix my gaze?"

"No, I— My apologies. I was staring. It is a heady thing to be so near the oracle queen."

"Yes. My crown blinds people to my faults. Maybe it will even blind your painter's eye, and my portrait will come out looking gorgeous." He looked down, and she felt guilty. What could he say to that? Flatter her and say she was beautiful? "An oracle queen is a queen like any other. Do not worry; I cannot spy into your heart and uncover your secrets."

"That is a relief. I must admit to knowing nothing about the sight gift. I have never traveled to Sunpool, and the gift outside of there is so rare."

"There is no shame in that. Being a poisoner is a mystery to me as well. All of the gifts are impossible to know to those who do not have them. You may ask me something if you like."

He paused in preparing his canvas and thought. "Did you always know you would win the crown?"

"I did. By the time the Ascension began after the Festival of Beltane, I had already had a strong, clear vision."

"Of your sisters' deaths?"

"Of myself. Wandering the rooms of the completed West Tower." She looked up at the Volroy, neck stretching back. She knew its silhouette well enough to see it with her eyes shut, where the unfinished tower ended and which stones jutted up like a gap-toothed smile.

"That must've been comforting," he said.

"It was. And it wasn't. The sight gift is many things, but I would never call it a comfort. Visions can be misinterpreted. They can be unavoidable, or they can be a warning."

Jonathan was silent a moment as his hand moved over the canvas and made small marks. His movements were exact and confident for an apprentice. Elsabet watched his eyes as they grew distant, studying the Volroy, and as they sharpened, focusing back on her face and gown.

"I would have this be a joyful portrait," she said. "A celebration of Midsummer. Nothing too dark."

"If you want it to be joyful, then you will have to smile." He raised his brow at her and chuckled. "Or I suppose I could simply imagine what that must look like." He stuck the handle of a brush between his teeth and went at the canvas with broad, dry-sounding strokes. Then he set the brushes aside and stepped back. "After you are set in the foreground, I will add things around you. Bushels of summer fruit and crops. I do a very fine set of playful hunting dogs."

Elsabet laughed. "You will make a naturalist of me."

"Not to worry. There is no mistaking an oracle queen in a portrait. Not with the aura of black shadow around her head." The aura of black. It was the traditional way of depicting the sight gift in paintings. The stronger the gift, the darker the aura. For a queen's portrait, it would be so dark it would appear to be a black orb floating just above her crown.

"Jugglers, then, and the feast table. I promise I will make it seem a very merry occasion."

"Then you must feast with us," she said. "So you may make an accurate representation."

Jonathan blushed, and Elsabet looked away. She had meant to get the measure of him, to find out why he had appeared in her dream. Instead, she was the one doing all the talking. More talking than she had done in years with anyone besides Rosamund and Bess.

"Well?" she asked. "What say you?"

"To an invitation from the queen?" He smiled, a pleased, befuddled expression on his face. "I can hardly refuse."

INDRID DOWN

❦

*T*he house that the Arrons kept in the capital stood on the north side, proud and darkly timbered. It had been built atop a small knoll and in the rear boasted a small walled garden full of poison. There, it got the best of the morning sun and the best of the breezes coming from the north end of the harbor before the wind made it to the market and began to reek of mingling foods and people. Unfortunately for Gilbert, it was also the council house that was the farthest away from the castle, and by journey's end on a warm summer day, the top of his forehead was beaded with sweat.

"I don't know why you won't settle in one of the row houses on High Street," he said as Francesca greeted him in the garden.

"I don't know why you won't ride a horse," she replied, and kissed his cheek.

"I told you; I don't care for horses. And my mount would too often be seen tied to your post."

Francesca laughed. "Your mount was seen often enough at my post when you first arrived in the capital." She slipped her hand below his tunic and squeezed, making him smile and flush. Their tryst had been sweet but brief. Over now for years. She had set her sights on him the moment he stepped out of the carriage behind the new queen. Seducing him had been easy; Gilbert had never been with a girl as lovely as Francesca Arron. For nearly two months, she had listened to his troubles with his head resting on her chest. Just long enough to learn his vulnerabilities. And his darkest desires to capitalize on.

Francesca shook her long, pale braid over her shoulder as he followed her to a stone table and flinched away from the plants.

"Can we go inside? I feel as if I could die from a deep breath in this garden."

"We do not keep poisons like that here." She bent to finish the letter she had been writing. "As long as you eat nothing and do not roll in anything, you will be fine."

"Roll in anything," he muttered, and tugged his sleeves in tighter. "What's that there?" He pointed to a small vine-covered stone set inside a tiny box of iron fence. "I've never seen that before."

Francesca glanced up to where he was pointing. "It's a grave marker, of course. It's usually obstructed and overgrown."

Gilbert walked closer and bent to read the engraving. Grave markers were rare on the island, as most bodies were burned on the pyre and the ashes scattered. Families kept woven shrouds as commemoration, or plaques, or engraved brick, but an actual grave was an uncommonly curious thing. Leave it to Gilbert to find it, with that strange manifestation of his sight gift.

"It's only engraved with the year. Who is it?"

"A long-ago child," Francesca replied. "She was legion-cursed and put to death in the temple here when she was nine. The poor thing. There are few easy deaths for a poisoner. Fewer merciful options when poison is not one of them." She handed her letter to a servant, along with her ink and pen, then sighed, staring at the grave. "They took off her head," she said, and Gilbert winced. "The family had her buried here unburned, holding it like a basket on her chest."

"Beheading is a cruel thing for a child," he agreed. "But still far kinder than leaving her to grow into the curse and to run mad."

"To be sure." She rubbed a bit of ink between her fingers and then clapped her hands. At a flick of her wrist, a silver vial appeared in her palm. "I have made it stronger this time."

"Stronger? Why?"

"Why? How can you ask why? You have been at the Black Council meetings. You have been at the court. She is still not listening to us. Still taking no guidance from her advisers."

He clenched his fist on the vial. She could see that he wanted to throw it. But he would not. Much as Gilbert loved the queen, he knew that her free spirit occasionally went too wide of tradition. And besides, he would never go against Francesca. Not after she had used her poison craft to weaken his older sister so that his position on the council was secured.

"Is it safe?"

Francesca's mouth fell open, her large blue eyes the picture of hurt. "How can you ask me that? Of course it is safe. A strong gift has made the queen too sure of herself. Too certain she knows what is best. With her gift muted, she will learn to rely on her friends. Really, it is for her own good."

"It's not even her fault. The Goddess gave her the sight to put her on the throne. And now we play with that like it is not a sacred thing. We could be leaving ourselves vulnerable to attack!"

Francesca clucked her tongue. "We still have your gift of sight."

"My gift is not the same as the queen's."

"But it will do for now." She pressed the vial harder into his palm and his hand down to his tied purse to hide it in.

"It's not forever," he said, and turned to go.

Not forever. Just until she learned to rely on her council. And on Francesca in particular. Francesca ran her tongue across her teeth and sipped a cup of unsweetened May wine. Poisoning the queen, even nonlethally, was a very dangerous game. And she was relying on soft-hearted Gilbert Lermont to play so much of it. With one hand, Francesca held the queen's gift down, as if underwater. And with the other, she aroused unrest and directed it toward the queen, by stoking Sonia Beaulin's warrior jealousy and whispering about the excessive costs associated with the construction of the castle. But still Elsabet did not turn to her as head of council. Still, that designation stayed vacant. And Francesca was running out of hands.

Just as that thought crossed her mind, a new set of hands slipped around her waist from behind. She smiled as the king-consort nibbled on her earlobe.

"Here you are, my beauty," he said. "What did that milksop want?"

"Never mind him." She turned in his arms and kissed him. "But it was a good thing you were not seen. You should return to the Volroy soon, before she sends out riders to search for you." Not that those riders would ever think to look at the Arron house, but she did not wish to press her luck. The king-consort had been spending more and more nights and afternoons. Too many. And even after long hours in her bed, he never seemed to want to leave.

"If I were free, I would never return to her," William said, his eyes bitter and faraway. "Not to a woman who had the gall to shame me before the court. Who put me on bended knee and forced me to beg and wheedle my way back into her bed! As if that were anywhere I wanted to be."

The loyalist in Francesca winced at the coldness of his words. He should not speak so of the queen. Not even a queen so foolish as this one. But outwardly, she smiled and touched his face.

"You should not seek to anger her. We need your charms to brighten the court."

"My charms are what anger her in the first place. I am to give no girl the slightest bit of attention or Elsabet will breathe fire. That is over now, in any case. If I have you in my bed, I have no need of any others."

"No." Francesca gently but firmly slipped out of his grasp and stood, her back to him. "You have an even greater need of others. You must spread your attentions like you never have before, in order to keep all suspicion from falling onto us."

"Of course."

Francesca smiled. The king-consort was Elsabet's weakest point. Let him flirt right under her nose. Let him drive her mad with it. He could be the distraction Francesca sought, and with the queen focused on keeping her husband in one place, she would be far too busy to interfere with Black Council business.

THE FESTIVAL OF MIDSUMMER

Queen Elsabet presided over the Midsummer festivities from a high seat in the courtyard. It was her one concession to the Black Council, to keep up and away from the raucous, celebrating crowds, but even though it had been only one, she wished she had fought harder. She did not want to be seen so high, so aloof. She wanted to mix with her subjects in times of peace.

"Wake up!"

Both Elsabet and Bess startled at Rosamund's voice. She was barking at one of the queensguard stationed just behind them.

"I was awake, Commander," the soldier said, and the sound they heard next was Rosamund cuffing the girl on the back of the head.

"Not awake enough. Rotate out if you can't be alert. On today of all days, when the queen is surrounded by strangers."

Teeth bared and grinding, Rosamund stepped into view, and Elsabet and Bess startled for a new reason. Her head of queensguard had gold and silver ribbons braided into her hair.

"Rosamund!" Bess exclaimed. "You look lovely!"

"Thank you!" Rosamund preened as her mood quickly shifted. "Though never as lovely as you, Bess."

Bess laughed, equally beautiful in a dress of deep green. Sometimes Elsabet thought she should find some new, less beautiful friends. Standing beside Bess and Rosamund constantly was certainly not doing her any favors.

"You must have your eye on someone this Midsummer." Bess scanned the crowd for anyone who might be watching Rosamund with particular interest, but nearly everyone was. Rosamund was never without admirers. "Is it serious this time? Could it be a husband? Or a blade-woman?"

"I won't settle until my service to the queen has ended. I can't imagine looking after these soft soldiers and my own little ones besides." She sighed. "Though I do sometimes yearn for soft little fingers curling round my own. And for the pain of childbirth!"

Elsabet laughed. "Only the war-gifted."

"I wish I were war-gifted," said Bess, "so I wouldn't fear it so."

Rosamund chuckled and half turned to the soldier she had admonished for dozing. "Did you think I was in jest? Rotate out! And keep yourself off my detail for the rest of the month."

"Yes, Commander."

Elsabet gave the girl a sympathetic smile as she bowed and watched her tromp sadly down the steps. "You know they would favor you more if you tried a softer touch, Rosamund."

"They would. And also if I bribed them with luxuries, like Sonia Beaulin. Beaulin thinks it a popularity contest, but I don't need to win their favor. These are your private queensguard. They are no mere army soldier; they are the best of the best! I expect so, and I will treat them accordingly."

"Even on a festival day, when I am in no danger?"

"To a queensguard soldier there is always danger. And as for festivals, I keep careful accounting of service. That girl served this Midsummer so she will not have to serve again next year, nor ever for two high festivals in a row." Rosamund straightened. "I am not unreasonable. And I don't appreciate your questions before the soldiers."

Bess's eyes widened, but Elsabet only laughed. "A queen may question what she will. But I am sorry, my friend. I should have known better."

She turned her attention back to the celebration, where the naturalists in attendance had begun to assemble their portion of the feast—the finest portion: gift-caught fish and a lovely roasted boar surrounded by apples so bright they appeared to be polished. Gilbert was directing which dishes would come to her in which order, his arms waving.

But the queen's gaze did not linger on Gilbert for long. She was looking for someone.

Bess leaned in close. "Who are you searching for?" It could

not be the king-consort. He had not left her sight line all day, after entering ceremoniously on her arm and promptly leaving her seemingly to court every pretty girl in attendance. The sight of him filled Elsabet with rage and shame. So she had resolved to ignore him.

"I am looking for someone I invited."

"Personally?" asked Rosamund.

"The painter. Jonathan Denton." But she did not see him. Perhaps he had only been polite when he had accepted her invitation. Perhaps she had frightened him away. Honestly, she did not know why she cared. She cleared her throat and glanced at her friends to see if they had noticed. But instead, both Bess and Rosamund were scowling down at the crowd.

"What's the matter?"

Bess blinked and forced a smile. "Don't think on it, Elsabet. No doubt he is just . . . in his cups."

Elsabet looked into the crowd. It did not take her long to find him. William. He had one arm around a pretty blond girl and his other around a brown-haired beauty, his fingers pulling the shoulder of her gown nearly down to her breast. In his cups, indeed. It was early evening; he had probably had eight glasses of festival wine and none of it adequately watered. Whatever the excuse, there he was: laughing, kissing their necks, and gifting them the rings off his fingers.

"Everyone can see this, can hear this," Elsabet murmured as her cheeks grew hot.

"I could send a blade," Rosamund said, taking a swallow

of wine against her own vow of festival sobriety. "Just to nick him."

"Ignore it," said Bess. "Pretend you don't see. Or don't care."

But it was too late for that. Already the whispers spread outward, until nearly every pair of eyes in the courtyard was darting between the king-consort and the queen. And what would they see? A weak queen who accepts her husband's infidelity, right under her nose?

Elsabet stood up suddenly. So suddenly that the girls in William's arms shuddered and tried to get away. But they were not her targets. The queen waited as the festival grew quiet. The musicians halted and servers froze half-leaned across banquet tables.

"William. My king-consort." She stopped. Waited for him to bow, as he should. As he must. "I tire of these festivities. Will you come now and preside over Midsummer, as is your sacred duty?"

"I will," he said, and began to make his way up to her. But when he leaned close for a kiss, she brushed him aside and stalked through the already muttering crowd. When she came face-to-face with the girls William had abandoned, she lost control of her temper and roared for them to get out of her way, unable to stand one more moment of their quivering, remorseful lips.

"Queen Elsabet," said Rosamund. "Where may we escort you?"

Elsabet grasped her arm. Already the anger and jealousy

were leaving her, and without them, she could not quite remember where she had meant to go.

And then she spotted him. Alone with a piece of bread in his forever paint-stained fingers, in the same clothes he had worn when she sat for her portrait. "There," she said, and went to him at once.

"Jonathan Denton," she said when he bowed. "Will you come with me to my chamber? I would have your update on the progress of my Midsummer portrait."

"I should not have done that."

Elsabet paced across the floor of her chamber. Her private chamber, where she and Jonathan were very alone.

"Did you see their eyes? Hear their whispers? They fear me. They think me volatile."

"They revere you. Fear and reverence can appear much the same."

Elsabet shook her head and did not pause her long, upset strides. "You are good to say that. But this is not the first time they have seen me lash out at that—that—!" She growled and threw up her hands. "And I shouted at those girls. As if it was their fault.

"And now, what will they say of you, Jonathan? Here, alone in the queen's chamber?"

He raised his eyebrows. "Let them say what they like. I am happy to be of whatever use to my queen as I can."

"No. I shouldn't have put you in this position. I will make

sure they know. That we were here discussing the portrait and nothing more!" She gestured vaguely toward his body. "I am not the kind of queen who takes revenge for infidelity by compelling some poor young man to . . . to . . ."

He chuckled. "It is all right, my queen."

She sighed and walked to her dressing table for a goblet of Gilbert's tonic, left over from that morning. The sight of William with his hands all over someone else had given her a headache.

"Is the wine no good?" Jonathan asked when she grimaced at the tonic's bitterness.

"It is not wine at all but a healing draught. I am well," she said before he could inquire, "but I sometimes get headaches."

Jonathan stepped toward her, sniffing the air. "May I?" he asked, and held out his hand. "I am a poisoner, as you know, and have a natural curiosity about the healing arts."

"Oh! Of course."

He stuck his nose in the cup and inhaled deeply, then took a sip, swirling before swallowing. He was silent for a long moment, staring into the last of the liquid. Then he frowned. "Where did you say you got this?"

"My foster brother, Gilbert Lermont. He has brought it to me for months. Why? Do you detect some interesting ingredient?"

"No."

"Or, with your interest in healing, would you recommend a different treatment?"

Jonathan looked at her. His eyes were troubled. "I would recommend that you stop taking this," he said.

Elsabet snorted. "Don't be ridiculous. Gilbert assures me—"

"At least let me take a sample."

He seemed so insistent, and she saw no harm, so she nodded. "Take whatever is left. I suppose, as a poisoner, you would know better than I."

"But with your gift of sight, surely you would know everything."

Her eyes widened, and so did his smile. "If only that were how it worked. Alas, I cannot even see whose bed my king-consort is falling into at night."

"He is a fool."

Elsabet cocked her head, and Jonathan lowered his eyes.

"Begging your pardon. I shouldn't have said that."

"What's said is said. Is that what all the people say? Do they think him a fool? Or me the fool for being wooed by his pretty face?"

"I'm afraid I don't hear much court gossip, with my nose inches from a canvas. The painting is coming along splendidly, by the way. I hope to be able to present it to you within a matter of weeks."

"Perhaps you could show me its progress."

"I would like that." His eyes took on a curious slant. "So you really don't hear all the gossip, then? I had heard that some oracles were able to hear the thoughts of others."

"Some can. The sight gift is varied and not well understood.

We are so rare. Even with me on the throne, the sight-gifted will never be as prolific as the naturalists or the elementals. What good would we be? The Goddess knows how best to balance her gifts." She motioned for him to take a seat and joined him, pouring some watered wine for them both to get the taste of Gilbert's tonic out of their mouths. "Sometimes the sight gift comes as nothing more than seeing cold spots. Violence and places of bloodshed."

"I know of that. I have read of it. 'Death leaves an impression as a cold stain upon the ground.'" His brow furrowed. "Is it like that for you?"

"Not only that, but yes. I can tell you the near-precise location where every queen before me died, for what feels like four generations. The places where my sisters died may as well be splashed with blood." She looked out her window. "How is your history? Do you know of Queen Elo, the fire breather, who burned a fleet of Selkan ships in Bardon Harbor?"

"I do. They say she put an end to foreign invasion, and in impressive fashion."

Elsabet smiled. Invasions would come again as new kings sought to leave their marks through conquest. But she had seen none coming during her time.

"I can hardly bear to look out into the harbor some days, depending on the wind," she said softly. "The churning ghosts are still so thick."

Jonathan swallowed and followed her gaze as if he might catch a glimpse of them himself.

"I don't tell that to many people," Elsabet said. "Bess knows. And sometimes I think Rosamund and Sonia—the war-gifted—can sense it. But I have never told them outright."

"Why not?" he asked, but then shook his head. "Forgive me. That was a foolish question. Seeing ghosts and scenting graves are shunned even in a fortune-teller. Of course they would be shunned in a queen."

"A queen is expected to yield grand prophecies. Not grow faint passing unmarked graveyards."

"Well. I find it a useful skill and would welcome you as a fellow traveler along unfamiliar roads."

He raised his cup to her, and Elsabet laughed.

"Every time we meet, I mean to find out more about you and instead give away more of myself. Do you inspire such candid conversation in everyone you meet, Jonathan Denton?"

"I'm sorry, my queen."

"Do not be sorry. Just do not become my enemy."

THE VOLROY

❧

Queen Elsabet and Bess walked along the rows of roses on the west side of the Volroy. To anyone watching, it would have looked like an idle errand: the queen accompanying her friend as she pruned. But those who knew her best knew that Bess was often the queen's eyes and ears, when she could not be seen to be looking or listening herself.

"You need better spies than me," Bess said quietly. "It is too well known I am of your household. No one speaks when I'm nearby."

"But who else could I trust? Only you and Rosamund." Perhaps Jonathan Denton, one day. But she did not say so out loud.

"Catherine Howe is loyal. And I am sure her household has very good spies." Bess clipped a rose and teased the petals back and forth beneath Elsabet's nose. "There was one rumor that was too loud to be hidden."

"What?"

"That Jonathan Denton is the queen's new lover."

Elsabet laughed. "New? As if there have been others." She had known that was what people would think. What she did not foresee was how much the idea would please her. "Poor Jonathan. He will have no peace."

"Poor Jonathan?" Bess smiled. "Is he coming back to the Volroy soon?"

"I think so." She prodded Bess in the hip when she laughed. "To show me my painting."

They walked together around the castle, and two servants stepped up and bowed.

"What's this?" she asked, and they held out a long, formal cape, soft and shining black. Threads of silver had been sewn into the collar.

"A gift for you, from the king-consort," one of the boys said.

Bess ran her fingers along the collar, thumb rubbing the silver. "It is very fine."

"He sends me gifts instead of returning to my bed. He sends me gifts with one hand while the other is inside some other woman's bodice." Her anger returned quickly. Her words took shape inside her head until she could see them, hear them, and she clenched her fists together and tore the cape along the seam.

"Take it! Get it away from me!"

The servants bowed their heads and ran, mumbling apologies.

"Elsabet." Bess put her hand on the queen's arm.

"Forgive me, Bess. I need no spies to know what the people

are saying about me. And what new things they will say about me now, following this outburst." She took a breath. "But I would know where my king-consort is spending so much of his time. Would you and Rosamund be kind enough to find out for me?"

Jonathan met Elsabet on the top floor of the West Tower as she spoke with her master builders about the progress of the construction. It was a hive of careful, deliberate activity as always, the air full of moving ropes and brick and stone. The clumsy poisoner boy nearly tripped twice and almost had his head taken off by a swinging board. Elsabet could barely contain her laughter as she watched him from the corner of her eye.

"This is coming along nicely," he said when he reached her, and bowed. He ran his hand along one of the interior walls, up the arch of the doorway to squeeze the keystone with his fingertips. The door led to a large chamber with several windows. "Will this be yours?"

"You could say the West Tower will be all mine. All of the queen's apartments contained within." She peered with him into the new space, still dusty from construction. "But no. My personal chambers are a floor below. Already complete. Perhaps I'll give these to my king-consort. Or perhaps not. I'd rather not hear him creeping past my floor on his way to . . . somewhere or other."

"In any case, the king-consort's rooms should be beneath the queen's."

Elsabet smiled. "What have you brought me?"

At the question, Jonathan ran back into the hall and returned with the covered canvas. He studied the light quickly before placing the easel to catch the soft afternoon sun. Then he uncovered the portrait.

Elsabet could hardly take it all in. It was as if he had taken Midsummer and made it tiny, such was the exactness of his rendering. The food piled high on the banquet table looked good enough to eat. And she even remembered seeing those exact familiar-dogs, brown-and-white with curling tails, a pair of them seated with great composure to one side, awaiting scraps.

The Volroy rose up in the background, a dark, majestic giant, even as the black stones were kissed with summer light.

"You have placed me down among them, not high up on a dais," Elsabet said.

"I thought you would prefer that. It—it suited the composition."

She nodded. It was the most accurate representation she had ever seen of herself. No great beauty. He had not embellished or softened her features. Yet somehow he had captured the air of her, the spirit. He made her eyes warm and sparkling, her expression confident and capable. She was, in his eyes, a handsome queen.

"The Volroy is unfinished, as you can see. I wanted to await your instruction, on how it should be depicted."

"Good," she said. "In due time. There is no hurry." Her fingers floated above the canvas. He did not need to ask whether she was pleased. She had not smiled so broadly in weeks.

"My queen, there was something else."

"Please, Jonathan, call me by my name. I give you leave."

"Queen Elsabet," he amended, and blushed. "There was something else. Have you . . . Has there been any noticeable weakening of your sight gift?"

"What?"

"Forgive me," he said quickly. "It is just that I have been evaluating the ingredients of the tonic you take, and I believe it may be harmful to you. And your gift."

Elsabet turned away from the painting. "That's not possible. The tonic comes from Gilbert. I'm sure you're mistaken."

"Of course. Though perhaps he is as well? He is not a poisoner; he would not know. Do you know where he got it? Would you allow me to investigate the matter further?"

Elsabet blinked. It made no sense, what he was saying. Gilbert would never harm her. Her gift was sacred to him. And he was her foster brother. Her only family. "There must be an explanation."

"Of course."

"And my gift is not gone," she said, lowering her voice. "I had a vision, not long ago. Well, not a vision, I suppose. But a dream."

"A dream? Is that common?"

"No. But it has proven true, and that is all that matters." She watched him from the corner of her eye. "I dreamed of you, Jonathan Denton. I knew you before we met."

INDRID DOWN

❧

When Rosamund opened the door to her family home, she found Catherine Howe, her head covered by a dark hood.

"Is the maid here already?" Catherine asked as Rosamund motioned for her to come inside.

"She is. Though we didn't expect you to be so quick."

Catherine took her hood down and shook out her pretty brown-gold curls. "When someone asks for information from the Howe spies, it is never long in coming."

"Very well," said Rosamund. "Bess is waiting down this way."

They had taken only a few steps when three little girls ran squealing past, batting at each other with small wooden swords, and knocked Catherine up against the wall. They were so frenzied and focused on their battle play that they clogged the narrow hall, and Rosamund had to scoop up the smallest one and put her on her shoulders in order to let them pass.

"My apologies," Rosamund said, and then laughed as the little girl beat her about the head with the wooden sword butt. "It is often this way in an Antere house."

Catherine squinted up at the little girl as she bashed Rosamund's skull. "Doesn't that hurt?"

"A little." Rosamund reached up and prodded the child in the ribs until she surrendered in peals of laughter. Once they cleared the hall, the girl slipped down and tore off in the other direction to rejoin the game. Rosamund gestured through a doorway. Inside, Bess was already waiting, seated at a table before a bottle of whiskey and three cups.

"Shouldn't you close the door?" Catherine asked, looking behind them.

"Are you so afraid of a few little warriors?" Rosamund chuckled. "Never mind about the door. My mother is resting and my brothers are deep into a card game in the kitchen with their wives. And besides, all are loyal."

"To you or to the queen?"

"To both," Rosamund said, her voice sharp. "So we may speak freely."

"Sit, Catherine," Bess said, and poured her a cup. "Take some to ease your nerves. Or would you prefer wine?"

Rosamund placed her hand on Bess's shoulder and planted her in her chair. "You sit. You are not a serving maid here, Bess, but a member of a ring of spies."

Bess exhaled and pressed her cheek against the warrior's

fingers. "I know that. But we should still make her feel at ease. She is quite distressed."

"I've noticed." Every candle in the room had been burning higher since Catherine entered. And having known Catherine since even before her time on the Black Council, Rosamund knew that her talent was for the element of earth. She must be nervous indeed to affect the flames so.

"Come now, Catherine. You can't have found anything that troubling over the course of so few days!"

Catherine's lips pressed together. "But I have. And it was not only over the last few days. My spies have been moving for months."

"Months?" Bess gasped. "But why?"

"We elementals are better at detecting shifting sentiments upon the air," Catherine replied. "Since I came to the Black Council, I have always kept a bird or two circling. I would always know what is being said of the queen."

Rosamund drank and refilled her cup. "And what is being said?"

"At first, that the queen was frivolous. Changeable. That she did not listen to her advisers, which in truth, she does not often."

"The queen follows her own mind," Rosamund snapped.

"Yes. In everything. And it has not gone unnoticed. The people, and the Black Council, have become accustomed to war queens, who command raids and battle and leave the governance to those better suited to it. Elsabet has taken some of that back."

"Is that not her right as queen?" Bess asked.

"Whether it is her right or not, it has embittered the council. I suspect that someone has been planting rumors amongst the people of the queen's foolishness. I even suspect that the king-consort may have a role to play, driving her to jealous outbursts in public."

"To what end?" Rosamund asked. "To make her unpopular?"

"To undermine her. I do not know, truly, what their aims are. But I fear for the queen's reputation and the recklessness of those whom I suspect."

"Out with it, then. Whom do you suspect?"

Catherine's delicate features pinched together. Her complexion was just a bit too tan to ever show a flush, but had she been only a little lighter, Rosamund was sure her whole face would have appeared bright red. "I am using measured words," she said, speaking slowly as if Rosamund were hard of understanding, "because I am not sure. But if I am right, then I am also sure that there is no limit to how far these people will go."

"What people?" Bess leaned forward and grasped Catherine by the hands. When Catherine still hesitated, Rosamund slammed her fist down, rattling the cups.

"What people? Enough games. We came to you. You know we can be trusted."

Catherine drained her whiskey and set the empty cup aside. "Last night, two of my spies were in the king-consort's party of an evening."

Bess's eyes widened. "Your spies lay with the king-consort?"

"Many of my spies have lain with the king-consort," Catherine said. "I keep many comely spies."

"Unimportant," said Rosamund. "What did they see?"

"They retired with him in an inn, seemingly for the night. Once there, he proceeded to get them more and more intoxicated on ale until they fell asleep. One of them awoke when he crept from the room, and followed him."

"Where did he go?"

"Not far. Another room. The girl was able to spy inside and able to listen. According to her, what was taking place inside the room was unmistakable." Catherine paused so the three of them could trade sour expressions. "She waited, hidden, until nearly dawn, when the king-consort and his paramour left. The woman was dressed commonly, but my girl swears that beneath the common serving clothes was none other than Francesca Arron."

Bess sank back in her chair. "A member of her own Black Council."

Rosamund sank back as well and ran her hand roughly across her face. "And a foolish member at that. Francesca Arron will lose her head for this and for what? A good-looking boy?"

Bess's eyes widened. "Rosamund, you don't think that Elsabet will have her executed?"

"Francesca is a member of her own Black Council, as you said. The queen cannot let it stand."

"Unless it could be kept secret—quiet—if perhaps Francesca

would beg forgiveness and swear to stay away from the king-consort—"

"You are both missing the point!" Catherine Howe pushed away from the table, and every candle flared. "If Francesca Arron is involved, it is not about one good-looking boy! She is only using him to further her own ends!"

"And what would those be?" Bess asked.

"I do not know," Catherine replied gravely.

"It doesn't matter." Rosamund poured whiskey up to the rim of her cup. "Elsabet is the Queen Crowned, and there is nothing Francesca Arron or anyone else can do about that. And whatever her plans may have been, we have found her out. We'll go to Elsabet. Surround her with loyalists. You and I, Bess and Gilbert. And I will be ready to arrest Francesca as soon as our queen gives the order."

Catherine looked at Rosamund curiously. "You are Elsabet's friend. Are you not afraid?"

Rosamund bared her teeth and snorted. "What is there to fear? She's the queen. It's not as if they can kill her."

THE VOLROY

❧

*F*rancesca Arron waited in the shadows of the Volroy until the painter finally emerged from his audience with the queen. It was late, near dusk, and his serene face was lit by candles and torches. It was clear to anyone watching how besotted he was with her. How pleased he was that she was pleased with him. He was so transparent and unguarded. A poisoner ought to have a more natural ability for subterfuge.

"Young master Denton."

The boy looked up and smiled, a dazzling smile in a mediocre face, beneath hair as dark as soiled straw. "Mistress Arron."

"I thought that was you," she said, and stepped out. "I was almost unsure. You have spent so much time at the castle of late that you seem practically a different person. If not for the pigment stains and oils beneath your fingernails, I might have missed you completely."

Jonathan glanced at his fingers and hid them behind his hip. "Is there something I can do for you, mistress?"

"Perhaps you could escort me to my carriage. It is late, and we are both leaving. . . ."

"Of course." He bowed and waited for her to walk a half step ahead.

"All this time you are spending with our queen cannot leave you much time for painting."

"But that is why I'm here. To update the queen on my progress."

"And what of the night spent in her chamber?" She laughed lightly at the look upon his face. "Word travels quickly." Francesca squared her shoulders and tossed her light blond braid. Her strides were long when she walked, and he was a bit winded by the time they neared the gates and the waiting carriages. It was a wonder he could keep pace with Elsabet, whose legs and strides were even longer.

"Well then, good evening, Jonathan. I imagine I will be seeing much more of you, now that the queen has decided to keep you as a new pet."

"A new pet?"

She watched carefully for a flash of malice in his eyes, but she could detect none. So perhaps he was more skilled at concealment than she had given him credit for.

"Of course. Ruling is such a strain upon the queen's person. She often seeks diversion. I hope you had not thought it something more."

Jonathan's smile faltered. "Are you trying to say you would prefer I spent less time here?"

"Not I," she said. "Were it up to me, Queen Elsabet could

take her meals with you in her lap. But some question your suitability as a queen's companion."

"Mistress Arron," he said with surprising vigor, "I am glad to know you're not among them. No doubt you are happy that Elsabet is keeping company with another of the poisoner gift." He drew himself up and straightened his shoulders. Francesca stifled a laugh.

"Who are you?" she asked. "A Denton? What great thing has the Denton house ever done for the island? For the poisoners? If you hope to make a place for that name within the capital, your hopes will be dashed." She stepped close and dragged her fingernail gently along his temple and the side of his jaw. "Arrons sit upon the Black Council. Arrons hold the political favor of the queen. And do not forget it."

Then she turned, unaffected by the shade of red he turned. Or the way his eyes bulged in impotent fury.

"You speak of it as though it is a permanent appointment," he said. "But members of the Black Council can be replaced. Perhaps the queen will be moved to have more poisoners in her circle now that she fears the tonic she takes for her health may have been unduly tainted."

She froze but as always was unshakable. Instead, she stared at the boy, stared and stared until he lost his nerve and turned away, cursing, and she watched him go, ascertaining just what to do with Jonathan Denton. Whether he could be bought. Whether he could be threatened.

INDRID DOWN

❧

*B*y the time Sonia Beaulin received her summons and met Francesca at the inn, it was the middle of the night. Which suited Francesca just fine. It meant that the inn was empty, except for the woman who ran it, and she was bought and paid for by Arron bribes. And it meant that Sonia was not likely to be seen walking through the central square, where it was always difficult not to be noticed. Warriors were like that. Brutal. Imposing. They liked to be noticed. A strange sort of people all around, in Francesca's opinion, moving things with their minds and always intent on blood. And unlike poisoners, who all appeared to be cut of the same cloth—thin, willowy people with a stern countenance and fair hair—warriors varied in shape and feature. Some were behemoths like the Commander of the Queensguard, Rosamund Antere. Others were so small and quick they could pass for very deadly children. Sonia fell somewhere in between, a slim-hipped, even-featured young woman with large observant eyes and hair nearly as dark as a queen's. Francesca preferred Sonia's more average size, as it made it easier to blend in, and she valued the possibility of underestimation. But Sonia envied Rosamund her height. It was yet another source of animosity between them.

Sonia slid into the secluded table where Francesca sat near the back of the inn and signaled to the innkeeper. "Whiskey," she ordered.

Francesca shook her head. "Ale. Keep your wits about you."

Sonia changed her request and sighed. "What's happened?"

"Less important than what has happened is what we must do." Francesca was drinking tea and dropped a sugar cube tainted with arsenic into her cup. The cube had been dyed bright green, to keep any non-poisoner customers from falling over dead. The presence of poisoner fare on the menu—even before the bribes started—was the reason she had chosen to patronize the inn on Highborne Street in the first place. It was one of the few establishments in the capital to consistently offer poisoned food.

"Queen Elsabet may soon come to suspect us."

"How? Have her visions returned? Is she not taking the tonic?"

"She may no longer trust the tonic."

"Then you must administer it some other way. Sneak it into her food. Aren't you poisoners good at that?"

"Terribly good. But the dosage is important. Too little and it will have no effect at all. Too much and it will kill her."

The innkeeper arrived with Sonia's ale and also a loaf of bread and some cheese. Sonia thanked her sullenly. "Well," she said, "she'll find no evidence. Her suspicion will cost us, though, of that you can be sure. This queen is vindictive. One or both of us are sure to lose our council seats."

Francesca's jaw tightened as she watched Sonia pout and eat, stuffing bread and cheese into her cheeks like a squirrel. It made her want to douse her in poisoned tea, force arsenic sugar down her throat. And she would have, if she did not have need of Sonia's might.

"Is that the way a warrior speaks? So easily of defeat?"

Sonia stopped chewing and spat bread onto the floor. "What, then, would you have me say? What would you have me do?"

"Nothing that you lack the nerve for."

Sonia sat for a moment. Then she laughed. "Stop goading me. There's no need. The Beaulins tied their fortune to the Arron carriage long before you and I. Say what it is that *you* have the nerve to do."

"I have grown up around enough snakes to know," Francesca said, "that the one who survives is the one who strikes first. So we will strike first. And perhaps we can put an end to this before word of our involvement ever reaches the queen."

That night, just before sunrise, Jonathan was wakened by a rap at his door. Groggy, he got out of bed and wrapped himself in a robe. He tried to light a candle, but his drowsy fingers made a mess of the match, and after the insistent knock sounded again, he gave up and went to answer in the dark.

He had no idea who it could be. He had few acquaintances in town who knew the location of his small apartment, and none who would call at such an hour. And the knock came not from the main door that led downstairs to the bakery owned by his landlord but from the side entrance in the alley.

Had he been more fully awake he might have used more caution when opening the door. He might have first asked who it was. But he was not, and so he turned the lock and threw up the latch. The word "who" had barely passed his lips before the hooded figure shoved past him into his drafty hall.

"Who are you? What is this?" he demanded, and his hand searched the table near the entry for something, anything to use as a weapon.

"Quiet, Jonathan. I come on behalf of the queen! I am her maid Bess."

In the dim light, he could not make out her face, but he detected the movement of her cloak hood lowering.

"Bess?" he asked. They had not spoken often, but he had seen her at the Volroy, a near-constant presence at Queen Elsabet's side.

"Yes."

"What are you doing here?" He stepped carefully past her and went back to retrieve the candle, which he lit easily enough now that he had been startled alert. He turned with it and saw Bess, dressed in a long, brown traveling cloak that was just a bit too large for her. She seemed agitated, out of breath and pacing. "Do you . . . bear a message?" He held out his hand.

"If I did, it would not be written," she said, and slapped it gently away.

"Of course." He wiped his face roughly with both hands, trying to quicken his wits. "Is the queen all right?"

"Do you have reason to think she would not be?"

"No. Only you here, pacing back and forth and looking like a wolf is on your trail."

Bess stopped pacing. She took a deep breath. Then she smiled at him, such a warm and fetching smile that he could not help but return it.

"I'm sorry," she said. "I shouldn't have frightened you like this. I shouldn't have even come here. But—"

"But what?"

"The night you spent in the queen's chamber." Bess spoke in a rush. Color rose into her cheeks before she could get all her words out. "Did you . . . have you . . . are you as they say? Are you the queen's lover?"

"No—no! I swear it!"

"I am her closest friend and confidante. You must tell me the truth."

"It is the truth, Bess. That night we talked. And she . . . I have come to care for her. As more than just my queen. But we didn't—she wouldn't—"

Somehow, his declaration seemed to make things worse. Bess's hands flew to her face, and she began to moan. "I wish that she had! My poor queen! And you are only her painter! Not a lover at all!"

"No, not a—" he said, and placed his hands on her arms to

calm her, "not that. But I would like to think I am not only a painter. I would like to think that I too am her friend."

"You may need to prove that." Bess wiped at her eyes. "Elsabet does not have easy days ahead. She will need us. All of us." Morning was beginning to creep over the city, and her eyes widened at the sight of his nightclothes. "I shouldn't have come. Forgive me." She made to reach for the door, and he stopped her and instead drew her farther inside.

"Bess, wait. Please stay a moment and sit. Tell me what you meant about the queen. Why will she suffer? What's the matter?" Bess nodded, and let herself be led to his table and two lonely chairs. "Your hands are like ice."

"There was a chill in the air tonight, from the water. And I haven't slept. I hope the queen is sleeping now. . . ."

Jonathan stoked his small fire back to life and swung a pot of water over it to heat for tea. "A warm cup will put you to rights." He searched his cupboard. "I don't know if I have untainted sugar. I have untainted honey; will that do?"

After the tea had steeped, he got it into her hands and waited as she sipped.

"You and I and Rosamund," she whispered. "Catherine Howe. Gilbert Lermont. We may be the only loyalists the queen has left. I don't want to believe that, but—"

"Why do you think so, Bess?"

She shook her head. "To tell you would be to place you in danger."

"Then let me place myself there." He took her by the hand.

"I suspect that Francesca Arron has somehow been poisoning the queen's tonic."

Bess's eyes widened. He knew by the expression on her face that Francesca Arron was also the one whom she suspected.

"I was near to the queen when she took her nightly dose," he explained. "And I am a poisoner and curious about healing. I asked her if I could take a sip, and she consented. And instantly, I knew that something was amiss."

"Are . . . are you sure?"

"The Dentons have little to recommend them, but we are excellent apothecaries. I am certain. I even took a sample to my family in Prynn."

Bess stood and set down her teacup hurriedly, sloshing tea over the rim. "I must go and tell the queen of this. I must tell Gilbert."

"I'll come with you," he said, and looked down at his nightclothes. "Just let me get dressed."

Bess put her hand on his chest. "No. You must stay here. This will all move very quickly, Jonathan, and if what you say is true and what we believe is true, then it is better if no one see us together yet. Rosamund—Commander Antere—does not want to alert Francesca to our suspicions."

Jonathan thought of his conversation with Francesca the night before. "She may already suspect me."

"All the more reason for you to stay away. The queen will send for you soon, I am sure. She will send for you when it is over and Francesca has been arrested."

"Bess," he said when her hand was on the door. "Tell the queen . . . tell the queen I am thinking of her."

"I will, Jonathan." Bess glanced toward the windows in his bedroom. "It's later than I thought. I should go." She stepped out as he held the door for her; she took his hand and squeezed it. "It will be all right."

He closed the door and wandered back into his room. Not knowing what else to do, he cleaned up the tea and dressed, readying himself for the day. But time had never moved so slowly. He could not stop thinking of what was happening at the Volroy. Of Elsabet and how he might be of help to her. "Blast," he said, and stood. "I cannot just wait."

He threw open his door and went down the steps, hurrying up the alley toward the square. Bess might frown when she saw him, but Elsabet would not be angry. And besides, if it was as Bess said, Elsabet needed all the friends around her that could be summoned.

When he turned the corner into the square, he stopped short. A crowd was gathering across the street. People, standing around and staring at something on the ground. His heart thumped as he walked closer and elbowed his way through. Then he saw the edge of her brown cloak.

Bess lay on the stone street, facedown, her arms at her sides. The arrow that had killed her stuck straight out of the back of her head, pinioning her cloak hood to her skull.

"Bess!" He fell to her side and turned her over. Her face was broken and bleeding from striking the stones when she fell. Her pretty eyes stared at the sky, and as he held her, blood soaked through her red-gold hair and into the hood. He drew the cloak hood back slightly and moaned. Whoever had done it had been a fine shot.

"Poor girl," the woman muttered. "Such a lovely thing. Who would think to do it on such a morning?" She looked at Jonathan sadly as he wept. "Was she with you, young man?"

"Elsabet," Jonathan croaked. Then he set Bess gently down. He got to his feet and ran for the Volroy, wiping her blood onto his tunic.

"Wonderful," Sonia said sarcastically to Francesca as they watched the Denton boy fuss over the dead maid. "We've killed the wrong commoner."

"*You* killed the wrong commoner," Francesca corrected.

"What was she doing, leaving his apartment at this hour?" Sonia asked, and Francesca wanted to slap her. That did not matter. The girl was dead. The queen's dear friend. And someone would have to pay. "What do we do now?"

"Now," Francesca whispered angrily, "we use it."

Stepping out of the morning shadows, she drew her hood down nearly completely over her face. She walked lightly and quickly, moving through the back of the crowd, slipping between people in that way that was natural to all poisoners, that way that made it easy for them to sink a poisoned dagger into a thigh or drop a poison-coated berry into a drink. But that morning, it was poison of a different sort that needed to be spread.

"Oh," she murmured in a gentle voice. "That is one of the queen's girls. One of the queen's maids! And she was coming from the queen's lover's apartment!"

That was all it took. The people latched on to it and filled in the rest. "The queen is often jealous," someone said. "How foolish of the boy," said someone else. "But who could blame him? Look how lovely this girl was. Lovely as our queen is not. That's why she's so jealous in the first place. Poor queen. Poor girl."

"Poor queen? This is murder! Murder over a lover's tryst!"

Francesca smiled. When she returned to Sonia she nearly laughed as the two of them walked out of the square unnoticed.

"How did you know to do that?" Sonia asked.

"You know what they say. An Arron is ready for anything. Now let us go. Our plans have changed."

THE VOLROY

❧

lsabet ordered Bess's body brought to the Volroy. She ordered healers and priestesses to look upon it, to provide her with what answers they could. But there was only so much that could be told about an arrow to the back of the head.

"Get away from her, then," Elsabet said, and draped herself over her friend. Her cheeks were red and wet with tears. She kissed Bess's cold hands. "What good am I?" she asked, wiping her eyes. "What good is an oracle queen who cannot see enough to protect those she loves?"

Rosamund, Jonathan, and Gilbert stood by helplessly. They too were full of sorrow. Even Rosamund had wept when she heard the news. Wept and raged when she saw the arrow struck through Bess's pretty head. Now they were alone in the throne room, the healers dismissed, the priestesses' prayers said. No other members of the Black Council were brave enough to show their faces with Bess's body stretched out across the council table.

"How could this happen?" Elsabet stalked back and forth, long legs shaking.

"Elsie," Gilbert ventured softly. "Let me get you something."

"What, Gilbert? What do I need?"

"I don't know. I could summon your king-consort. He will want to know of this."

In the corner of her eye, Elsabet saw Rosamund bare her teeth.

"William?" Elsabet laughed. "He is hiding somewhere like the rat he is. He knows he does not need to put on an act anymore." She turned back to Bess and wiped her eyes again. "Where is Catherine Howe?" she demanded, voice booming.

"We don't know, Elsie. She is not yet at the Volroy this morning."

"Where is Sonia Beaulin?"

"She is here," Rosamund answered. "I don't know where just now, but I have seen her."

"Where is Francesca Arron?"

"We have not seen her yet this morning either."

Elsabet looked at Rosamund. "Things will move quickly now."

"Yes, my queen."

"What will move quickly now?" Gilbert asked. He had not heard the news that Rosamund had delivered to her that morning that thanks to Catherine Howe's spies, they knew her king-consort was betraying her with Francesca Arron. Nor had he heard the message of poisoned tonic that Jonathan had whispered into her ear.

"Then give me a moment alone with Jonathan."

Rosamund nodded and tugged a sputtering Gilbert from the room.

"My queen," said Jonathan, his shoulders square. "Queen Elsabet. What can I do to help you?"

"You can run."

"What?"

Elsabet wiped another tear from her cheek, the last she would allow herself to cry today. "The capital will not be safe for you for a time. Not even here in the Volroy. You must find a way to get out of the city before it begins."

"But"—he gestured sadly toward Bess—"it's already begun. I can't leave you, not now."

"You can and you must, because I order it. I have arranged for enough coin, and you will find a fast horse awaiting you in the stables."

"No," he said, and to her surprise, he came and took her by the shoulders. "I am supposed to be here. You dreamed of me. You dreamed of me so I could fight for you."

Elsabet smiled. She touched his face. How she wanted for that to be true.

"No, Jonathan. I dreamed of you for solace. So you could be a moment of peace for me when everything around me crumbled. But it was not a vision. It was only a dream."

* * *

After Jonathan had gone, Elsabet summoned Rosamund and Gilbert to return.

"Tell me," she said to them, "in your short time waiting in the halls, what are they saying? What are the whispers?"

"They are trying to say it was an accident," Rosamund muttered. "As if an arrow to the head can be an accident."

"It can be," Gilbert said softly. "It could be. Bess could have just been in the wrong place at the wrong time. It could have been a case of mistaken identity."

Elsabet looked at him sharply. "Now that I do not doubt. Covered in a heavy cloak in the early light of morning? Having just left Jonathan's apartment? Mistaken identity, indeed. That arrow was meant for him, and it found her instead."

Gilbert's lips trembled around his words, cautious, as if he feared whatever he said next could lead them down dangerous paths. "Who? Who would dare? Have you seen something?"

"Seen something? No, I have seen nothing." Elsabet closed her eyes, then opened them, fixed upon his face. "Though perhaps I could, if I were to have more of your tonic."

He twitched but did not speak. He did not confess. And that hurt her as much as anything else.

"Did you know, Gilbert? All this time that you were poisoning me, poisoning my sight gift right out of me, did you know?"

His lower lip wobbled, and he closed his eyes. "I had no choice."

"No choice?" Elsabet exploded. "No choice but to betray me? Your own foster sister? Who has loved you since we were children?"

"I had to. Francesca poisoned my way onto the council, and she swore she would poison me, too, or reveal my secret—"

"Francesca Arron does not give commands! I give commands! Francesca Arron does not rule! I rule! And you should have known better, Gilbert."

Gilbert dropped to his knees. He clasped his hands together. "Forgive me, Elsie. I never wanted to—"

"Be silent."

He tried to obey, though he began to weep. "What would you have of me? What can I do?"

"I don't know yet what I am going to do with you," Elsabet replied. "For now, get out of my sight. Return to your rooms and stay safe. Stay there under guard. Until this is over."

"This?" he asked.

"Go!" she roared, and he scurried from the room, so afraid of her that she would have laughed, had she not been so angry and heartbroken.

Finally, it was only she and Rosamund.

"What now, my queen?"

Elsabet looked at her friend, her warrior, her hair so blazing red and her reputation so fierce that rumors persisted of her dyeing it that way with madder root just to make it look like blood.

"You know what now," she said. "Now you take your queensguard and arrest Francesca Arron. Arrest her and throw her in the cells on charge of murder." Rosamund nodded grimly, and Elsabet bared her teeth. "Now we end it."

THE VOLROY

❧

"That is not going to happen."

Sonia Beaulin stepped into the throne room with a number of queensguard soldiers. They spilled in through the open doors and spread until they lined the walls and blocked every possible exit. And over Sonia's shoulder, Elsabet saw more. More and more, armed and ready to fight, clogging the castle with their black-and-silver armor.

"What is the meaning of this?" Elsabet demanded. But no one answered.

Rosamund strode forward. Her mere movement was enough to make the closest soldiers shrink back, though she had not even drawn her sword. "What do you think you're doing, Sonia?"

"What I must. What you could not. We are arresting a dangerous and murderous queen."

Elsabet's mouth dropped open. "Murderous? Who did

I murder?" Her voice grew angrier and louder as she spoke. "Bess? Do you mean to pin the assassination of my own dear friend on *me*?"

"Do not listen," Sonia ordered the soldiers. "The queen is unwell. Take her into custody now and into the West Tower. There she may be kept safe."

"Safe? Safe from whom?" Elsabet began to tremble as the soldiers swept past Rosamund. She was as still as stone until they first took her by the wrist, and then she erupted, screaming and cursing them, throwing herself back and forth.

"Safe from yourself, my queen," said Sonia as they dragged Elsabet past.

"You cannot do this to me! I am your queen! I am the Goddess's chosen! Rosamund!" She craned her neck, able to see her commander standing a head above the others, the expression on her face still and full of anger, disbelief, and shame as she watched her own soldiers take her queen away. "Rosamund?"

They moved her quickly, through the castle and up the many staircases to the newly furnished queen's apartments in the West Tower.

"Why do we not go to my chamber?" Elsabet asked. "I have not yet moved to these rooms!" She searched their faces. None spoke. All were afraid. But they did as they were told. They followed their orders. Only they were not meant to take orders from Sonia Beaulin or the Black Council. Not without Elsabet's approval.

When she saw the open door, she knew it for what it was: a

finely decorated prison. She dug her heels hard into the stones and struck out at the nearest queensguard, her vision blacking in and out with panic as they pushed her toward it.

"No! No, let me go!"

But they would not. They shoved her through the door so hard she stumbled and nearly fell to her knees, and by the time she turned back, the heavy wood was already swinging shut.

Rosamund stood silently in the middle of the throne room. Her eyes focused on no one in particular until she could no longer hear Elsabet's cries. Then she turned to Sonia.

The look on the other warrior's face nearly drove her to strike. So smug. So pleased with herself. She was proud of putting Rosamund in her place. Proud of being a traitor.

"How does it feel?" Sonia asked. "To know that your queensguard was never really yours? That they have been mine, all this time?"

"Not all of them."

Sonia sighed. "No. Not all. But those have been dealt with."

"What do you mean to do here, Sonia? What do you and Francesca have planned?" Her voice remained calm, almost weary. Almost bored. And with every word, a little of Sonia's joy was chipped away. "Or do you even know? Perhaps she does not tell you. The master often doesn't inform the puppet about the play." She raised her eyes to the gathered soldiers. Many were good. Many she had trusted. They were only afraid, and following orders, and being lied to. "I don't know what she has told you. Maybe she told you they would release the queen as soon as those who led her astray were dead. But you must know that is a lie. They can never let Elsabet out again, not without losing their heads."

"Shut your mouth," Sonia snapped.

"I won't have you lying to them. If they do this, they should know what it is they are doing. They are deposing a Queen Crowned." She waited. A small ripple of doubt passed through them, but it amounted to only a shuffling of feet and some hard, nervous swallows. Not that she had really expected more. She had truly just wanted them to know.

"Give up your sword, Rosamund, and come quietly. I'll put you in the very best of the cells, you have my word."

Rosamund stepped forward.

"You can't win." Sonia's eyes glittered. She drew her sword. "There is no point in trying. No point in fighting. The cause is lost. Already the soldiers have eliminated the Howes. They say Catherine and the rest of them burned up in a fire of their own making. And as for your house . . ."

Rosamund thought of Antere House. Her brothers, laughing in the kitchen, the wives planning some grand hunt. Her mother, old now and unwell, but still ruler of them all. And the girls. The sweet, wild girls who slept with their wooden swords in their arms like dolls and covered her face with kisses when she returned from the Volroy after a long day.

"You should not have told me about my house, Sonia."

"Why not?"

"Because now there is no one for me to protect by surrendering."

Rosamund drew her sword with a bellow and brought it arcing down directly at Sonia's head, so fast that the other warrior could not fully block it, and the blade glanced down along her arm, finding its way through her armor and drawing blood. Those who saw Rosamund fight always said it was a wonder she could move so fast, with her bulk and size. They said watching her was like watching a dance of red and silver.

Rosamund's sword clashed again with Sonia's, and she pressed up close as the other warrior glanced at the wide-eyed soldiers. "None of them will intervene. None have the stomach to face me outside of training. How many do you think are secretly hoping that I will win?"

Sonia growled and shoved her away. They met and clashed and fell back again, and it was clear whose war gift was the stronger. Sonia panted, soft from so long sitting on the Black Council. Rosamund's sword was light as a dagger in her hand.

"Stand down!" Sonia shouted, and threw three fast knives, guiding them with her gift. But Rosamund knocked them all away. Then she picked them up and sent them back, her own gift too strong to be deflected, so that Sonia had to dodge and duck.

"Sonia Beaulin, in your fine black cape and fancy, shining boots. Dressed up in a warrior's clothes with no war gift to speak of."

Teeth bared, Sonia charged, slashing and striking with all

her might. Together they stumbled into a table. They knocked up against the watching, astonished soldiers. She sliced into Rosamund's shoulder, and Rosamund fell across the long table and rolled, but came up on one knee and laughed when she saw Sonia panting.

"Weak," Rosamund said. "Pampered, Black Council pet."

Sonia leaped, and Rosamund blocked and kicked. Sonia spit blood onto the wood floor.

"You're too small for this, Beaulin. Why don't you send the rest of my army in here to finish what you can barely start?"

Sonia wiped her mouth on her sleeve. "You are truly mad," she said. "Your whole family is dead. They tell me your mother was stabbed in her bed."

"My mother would never die in bed." Rosamund bellowed and charged her again, metal on metal like a song in her ears and Sonia's frustration turning to fear like a song in her heart. Sonia pushed back with her gift; Rosamund felt it, like a hammer against her chest. But Rosamund's gift pushed back harder.

"Guards!" Sonia shouted, and they stepped forward like cautious dogs to surround Rosamund and Sonia in the center of the room.

"They won't follow you," Rosamund said, her smile full of red teeth, "unless you do it yourself."

"They already follow me," Sonia growled.

Rosamund fought as bravely as she could, for as long as she could. She cut down three, then four of her trusted soldiers. She ran them through. She knocked them back and sent them flying. But every one she dispatched was replaced by two, and the swords began to land. Blood ran down her arms, her legs; it spread across the floor. When Rosamund had gone down to one knee, Sonia finally came to finish her, and by then, there were too many knives in Rosamund's back to know which one it was.

Coward, Rosamund thought as the blood filled her lungs, as she dragged herself through the fury until she saw the toes of Sonia's fine, black boots. She had hardly any strength left, but she found enough to raise her dagger and stab Sonia through the foot. Sonia Beaulin screamed like a child and dropped to the ground.

And Rosamund Antere died with a smile on her face.

PRYNN

❧

*B*y the time he reached Prynn, Jonathan's horse was nearly spent, even though it was a fine mount gifted to him from the queen's stables. He supposed he had not been mindful and had ridden her too hard. He bent and patted her frothy neck. Rest and time in a good stable, with plenty of grain and cool water, and she would soon be back to herself. Fit enough to carry him . . . wherever he decided to disappear to.

Jonathan sighed. He did not know exactly what he had hoped his return to Prynn would be, but it was not this, creeping in under cover of dark, running, when everything inside him said to turn back and fight, turn back and protect Elsabet from whatever came. But what could he do? She was his queen, and he would obey.

The horse's tired steps clipped and clopped along the road. When he turned the corner of the street that led to his family's house, not one of the finest in Prynn but nor was it on beggars' row, his mood lightened, thinking of his mother, and his father, his sister, and her two little ones.

Beneath him, his horse snorted and pulled up short. She smelled the wrongness and blood before he was close enough to see the broken-in door. Jonathan leaped from the saddle and ran inside, even though the silence warned him against hope.

He found his mother first, in the dining room, propped up in a chair. The blood that soaked the front of her dress was still warm. His father lay nearby on the floor.

Jonathan walked through the house in a daze. The night air was cold on his skin and blew through in a constant current. Their home had been cracked open and ruined. When he found his sister lying across the stairs, he drew her into his lap and wept, and when the creak sounded behind him, he could not remember if it was only a noise from the house at night or if it meant someone else was still inside.

THE VOLROY

❦

They left Elsabet alone in her prison in the West Tower for one long day and a night. Long enough for her to pace herself exhausted and to scream herself hoarse. They brought food, and she dashed it against the walls. They sent maids to clean it, and she chased them back through the door. And all the while from her window, there appeared to be nothing amiss. No great assault by loyal queensguard on the Volroy. No uprising of her people gathered at the gates. Ships docked in the harbor and sailed away reloaded. Carriages passed in the streets. No one heard her shouting. No one missed her.

Finally, midmorning of the second day, the door opened, and Elsabet turned to see Francesca Arron standing inside. For a moment, she and the queen stared at each other. But it was Francesca who looked away first, to frown disapprovingly at the mess of food on the walls.

"That will rot," she said. "It will begin to smell if you do not let the maids clean it up. It is already starting to."

"They may clean it when I am free from here."

Francesca sighed. "You are not doing anything to help your-self. Screaming at the servants. Throwing food like a spoiled child. What are the people to believe when they hear such things? You are making this all very easy for me."

Elsabet narrowed her eyes. "What do you mean to do?"

"What I have already done. Imprisoned a dangerous queen, for her safety as well as the safety of the island."

"The safety of the island. I am its chosen! You cannot keep me here!" She wanted to slap Francesca Arron with all her strength. She wanted to choke her unconscious with her long, blond braid. "Where is Rosamund Antere?"

"Rosamund Antere?" Francesca asked. "Rosamund Antere is dead. So is Catherine Howe. And Bess, the maid. And your handsome friend Jonathan Denton."

Elsabet's mouth hung open. Rosamund and Jonathan dead? The words made no sense. "You lie."

Francesca walked farther into the room, inspecting the trap-pings, the fine royal pieces that the queen's chambers had been furnished with. She ran her hand across the dark wood table and touched the embroidered hanging on the wall. She even put her palm to the fire and inquired if it was hot enough or if it smoked.

"You lie, I said," Elsabet hissed. "Get out!"

"I do not lie," Francesca said gently. Her expression could change in the space of a moment. How had Elsabet ever thought she could be trusted on the council? "You are still upset. It was a monstrous thing, after all. I am not surprised if you don't remember . . . giving the order."

"What order?"

"The order to execute Catherine and your captain of the queensguard. You were so convinced of their treachery. And the soldiers could do nothing but obey. You are a queen of the sight gift, and their faith in you was absolute." Francesca clapped her hands free of soot and smiled her prettiest smile. "Of course the people are aghast that you would order such brutal executions without reason or investigation."

"No one will believe you," Elsabet growled. "I did none of these things. Bring me Rosamund Antere! I don't believe you that she is dead. If no one would stand against me, they would never dare stand against her."

"She is dead, my queen. She and her entire house. A whole house dead, and the Howes met a similar fate. And the Dentons, poor poisoner folk. They were perhaps the most innocent in this, simply in the wrong place at the wrong time, caught up in a queen's misguided wrath."

Elsabet's head spun with the falseness of the accusations. This could not be. None of it could stand that she, the queen, would be imprisoned in her own castle, her loyal friends murdered, her enemies left to rule in her place.

"You will not get away with this! I will see you on trial. I will see you hang."

Francesca laughed. "You will have a difficult time seeing

much of anything from up here in your tower." She smiled cruelly. "Elsabet, queen you will remain, but you will never come down from here again."

"What?"

"It is for your own safety as much as ours. I fear that, enraged as the people have become with you, they might tear you apart on sight."

Elsabet clenched her fists to keep from crying. She would not cry in front of Francesca. She would spit in her eye. She would scratch her face. "You can't keep me here, as a prisoner. I am your queen! I am the one who will bear the triplets!"

"Of course you are! I would not dream of keeping your king-consort from you. He will visit you regularly. When he is not with me."

Elsabet's face burned. "You are small and foolish indeed if you think I care about his fate after all this."

"Do not forsake what friends you have. Or you will be very lonely here."

"I will not be here. I will get out."

The poisoner sighed and clasped her hands in front of her skirt. "It will be easier on everyone if you accept your loss." She turned to leave, slipping out, and Elsabet charged the door and hammered against it with her hands and elbows.

"It will never be easy! I will never stop trying to get out of here, do you hear me? Never!"

Gilbert stared across the table at Catherine Howe's empty seat as the Black Council met to take stock of the ruin that had befallen the crown and the capital. Without Catherine, and without Elsabet, without Rosamund outside the door, the council chamber felt so empty. Sonia Beaulin was still there, of course. And for some reason the king-consort. And Francesca Arron had seated herself at the head.

He wanted to speak against that. As the queen's foster brother, the head of the Black Council should have fallen to him. But who could he speak to? He had let himself be surrounded by snakes.

"What is he doing here?" Gilbert asked, and gestured to the king-consort.

William smiled. "The kingdom is short on advisers, brother. You should count yourself lucky that I am here and ready to serve."

"The kingdom is not a kingdom at all," Gilbert said. "It is a queendom, and you will not forget it."

"Of course none of us will forget it." Francesca Arron cleared her throat. "Not even with the unfortunate madness that has taken over our queen."

"So unfortunate," Sonia echoed, and shifted her weight. She seemed to be having some discomfort, and Gilbert noticed she had walked into the room with a bad limp. Good Rosamund must have done that before she . . . He closed his eyes and shuddered.

"The people will not accept this," Gilbert ventured. "And it is dangerous. They will want their queen, or they will want to kill her, and—"

"They will never want to kill her." Francesca looked at him

sharply. "The queen is sacred. The queen's line is sacred, as it always has been. She will be kept and cared for, safe in her West Tower until the triplets come."

"Some will question—"

"They question *her*. They have heard the rumors of her jealousy. They know she has been secretly seeking out those she thought were betraying her."

"So Elsabet ordered the execution of Catherine Howe, whom she branded a traitor, and her own head of queensguard? What reason did she have to execute the Dentons? The house of her new favorite?"

Francesca pursed her lips. "The same reason she had to kill the maid. She saw the maid sneaking from the Denton boy's apartments and ordered the Denton boy killed when he fled."

Gilbert stared at her. "This is your plan? Your explanation? Your punishment of the queen, and for what? What great crime had she committed?" He narrowed his eyes at William. "That she sought to possess an unworthy consort?" He turned to Sonia. "That she did not appoint you Commander of Queensguard?" He glared at Francesca. "That she did not do as she was told?"

He pushed his chair back and stood. "I'll have no part in this," he said, and walked out. It was not long before he heard Francesca's soft, catlike footsteps behind him in the corridor.

"We both know you will return," she said. "When you have had enough of sorrow and come back to your senses." She placed gentle fingers on his shoulder and touched his face. "It is over. Elsabet lost. But the island still has need of you, Gilbert. And she will like it if you stay nearby."

"How could you do this?"

"I had no choice."

"No choice?"

"All I wanted was for her to listen. To be a good queen and rule properly, through my—our—advice. But what could I do after she sent her spies for me? Let myself be cornered? Let myself be hanged? I told you before: there are few merciful ways to put a poisoner to death. And so I fought instead." She patted his forearm and turned to go.

"Did you poison me, too?" he called after her. "Did you mute my gift as well as hers, without my knowing? Is that why I foresaw none of this?"

Francesca paused as if trying to decide whether to lie. Then she sighed.

"No, Gilbert, I did not poison you. In fact, I choose to think it was a sign from the Goddess that she sent you no warning. Perhaps this is"—she cocked her head—"what she meant to happen."

THE WEST TOWER

❧

*T*he maid set down the tray of bread and boiled eggs. She poured the water and a steaming cup of tea. "There you are, Queen Elsabet," she said as if the queen were a child. She set the cloth on Elsabet's lap and even tucked her hair behind her ear. "You're looking very pretty today. After you break your fast, we'll brush your hair and put on a new gown."

She began to hum, and Elsabet looked up at her as she ate. She had no appetite, but if she did not eat, then they would make her, and she lacked the energy to fight.

"You look a little bit like her," she said, and the maid barely looked up.

"Like who?"

"Like Bess." She did not, though, not really. Bess had been beautiful. Far more beautiful than this mouse of a girl, who had likely been chosen to serve due to her slowness of mind and lack of guile than for any true merit.

"Let's not speak of them now, my queen. You know how upset you get."

"Have they had the burnings yet?" Elsabet went on. "For the Dentons? Will they bring them here and burn them in the capital as I asked?"

"Queen Elsabet—"

"Tell me!"

The maid jumped and looked at her with wide eyes. Elsabet quickly smiled and sweetened her voice.

"Please. Tell me."

"I think the Dentons were all burned together in Prynn," she said. "That's what they say."

"They." Elsabet chuckled. "Always 'they.'"

There was a knock at the door, and the maid left eagerly to answer it. When she returned, she brought Gilbert hovering behind her.

"Here is Master Lermont to cheer you."

The maid left them alone, and Gilbert came and embraced her, kissing her on both cheeks. "Terrorizing her as usual, I see."

"I will never stop."

"It was not her fault."

"It was everyone's fault, Gilbert. Mine. Yours. You know it's true. That's why you keep coming back after I heap abuses on you. Out of guilt."

"Out of love, Elsie. Mainly out of love."

"What use have I for love in prison?" Elsabet took a last bite of egg and wiped her mouth. Then she gestured for him to sit. "What have you brought for me? What is that under your arm?"

Gilbert grinned and took her by the hand. He led her to her bedroom and began to unroll the package he carried, unfurling it so it lay across her coverlet.

"Something I think you'll like," he said. "Something I smuggled in."

Elsabet looked down and held her breath. It was Jonathan's painting, the portrait he did of her for Midsummer, laid out in vibrant colors, bright and green, with shining fruit and the jolly faces of the little dogs.

"I recovered it at his apartment before it was ransacked and searched. It really is quite lovely. He was . . . quite talented."

Elsabet stared at the painting and took Gilbert by the arm. What a perfect time Midsummer seemed to her now, after all that had happened. All that warmth and innocence. Looking into the painting, she could almost imagine herself back there again, with Bess at her side and Rosamund always looking out for danger.

She reached down and ran her fingers across the Volroy, whole and complete in the painting.

"He found the time to finish it," she whispered.

"What?" Gilbert turned and looked at her. "Oh, Elsie, I meant for it to please you. I thought you might like it."

Elsabet smiled and squeezed his arm. She wiped the tears from her cheek.

"I do like it, Gilbert. I love it."